"I've Ached for Days Wanting You."

In one sudden motion Jon swept Carole off her feet and strode to the bedroom, kicking open the door.

"No, Jon, not like this," she cried. "You used to know how—to perfection."

"Then show me," he challenged.

She loved him, and when she drew his lips to hers she tried to let her kiss tell him so.

He answered with such stunning sweetness that she felt herself turning to flame.

"Now," he laughed triumphantly, "I'm starting to remember. . . ."

ANNE LACEY
began writing as a child in the small Arkansas town where she was born. She currently lives and works in Texas, though she considers south Louisiana her spiritual home and would love to return. She is an exercise and health-food nut who loves to travel.

Dear Reader:

Silhouette has always tried to give you exactly what you want. When you asked for increased realism, deeper characterization and greater length, we brought you Silhouette Special Editions. When you asked for increased sensuality, we brought you Silhouette Desire. Now you ask for books with the length and depth of Special Editions, the sensuality of Desire, but with something else besides, something that no one else offers. Now we bring you SILHOUETTE INTIMATE MOMENTS, true romance novels, longer than the usual, with all the depth that length requires. More sensuous than the usual, with characters whose maturity matches that sensuality. Books with the ingredient no one else has tapped: excitement.

There is an electricity between two people in love that makes everything they do magic, larger than life—and this is what we bring you in SILHOUETTE INTIMATE MOMENTS. Look for them this May, wherever you buy books.

These books are for the woman who wants more than she has ever had before. These books are for you. As always, we look forward to your comments and suggestions. You can write to me at the address below:

Karen Solem
Editor-in-Chief
Silhouette Books
P.O. Box 769
New York, N.Y. 10019

ANNE LACEY
Love Feud

Silhouette Special Edition
Published by Silhouette Books New York
America's Publisher of Contemporary Romance

SILHOUETTE BOOKS, a Simon & Schuster Division of
GULF & WESTERN CORPORATION
1230 Avenue of the Americas, New York, N.Y. 10020

Distributed by Pocket Books

ISBN: 0-671-53593-5

First Silhouette Books printing May, 1983

10 9 8 7 6 5 4 3 2 1

Map by Ray Lundgren

SILHOUETTE, SILHOUETTE SPECIAL EDITION and
colophon are registered trademarks of Simon & Schuster.

America's Publisher of Contemporary Romance

Printed in the U.S.A.

For my best friend Carol, who heartens the world with her own happy song

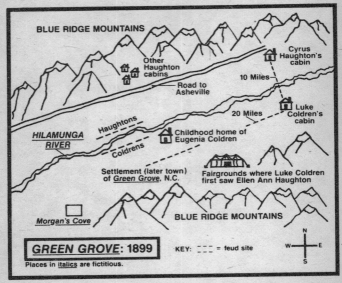

BLUE RIDGE MOUNTAINS

Other Haughton cabins

Cyrus Haughton's cabin

Road to Asheville

10 Miles

Luke Coldren's cabin

HILAMUNGA RIVER

Haughtons

Coldrens

20 Miles

Childhood home of Eugenia Coldren

Settlement (later town) of *Green Grove*, N.C.

Fairgrounds where Luke Coldren first saw Ellen Ann Haughton

Morgan's Cove

BLUE RIDGE MOUNTAINS

GREEN GROVE: 1899

KEY: --- = feud site

N W E S

Places in *italics* are fictitious.

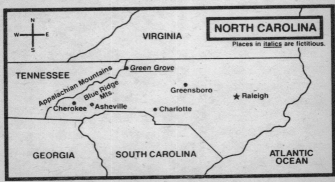

N W E S

NORTH CAROLINA

Places in *italics* are fictitious.

VIRGINIA

TENNESSEE

Appalachian Mountains

Blue Ridge Mts.

Green Grove

Cherokee

Asheville

Greensboro

Charlotte

★ Raleigh

GEORGIA

SOUTH CAROLINA

ATLANTIC OCEAN

Chapter One

The meadow was richly carpeted with wild-flowers of yellow, purple and white. It was a breathtaking sight against the clear, white-clouded sky and the hazy blue ridges of distant mountains, thick with virgin timber. But even a meadow of wildflowers grows boring when one has been staring at it for over an hour, as Carole Coldren had.

Impatiently she shifted her position, leaning against the fender of her compact car. For three days the little car had hummed and purred its way from Carole's home in Houston, Texas, through the flatlands and into the grandeur of the Appalachian Mountains, only to stall unexpectedly, cough and die a scant twenty miles from her destination, the little town of Green Grove in North Carolina.

At first Carole had tackled the problem with her usual aplomb. She turned the ignition on and off, stomped on the accelerator and swore aloud. When those measures failed, she debated raising the warm hood of the compact. She would have to stand well back in case any corrosive fluid spurted out and endangered the new blue denim pants suit she wore. The suit carried a designer label, as did the casual white pullover Carole had belted around her slim waist. She had chosen her wardrobe for this trip carefully, wanting to look smart and competent when facing her relatives in Green Grove again and, yes, anyone else—not, of course, that she really expected to see *him*.

Carole's mother had been amused at the trouble her daughter took in packing her two suitcases. "Really, darling, why try to impress a bunch of barefoot hillbillies?"

"They aren't hillbillies," Carole replied, shaking out the folds of a low-cut white sundress.

"Nonsense," Marsha Coldren scoffed. "Your father told me all about them. Living back in those hollows and woods with hound dogs, outhouses and stills, riding mules, shooting up the countryside—and each other!" Marsha shuddered. She was city-born and never happy unless she lived a few blocks from a multilevel mall.

"Mother, that was in the Dark Ages," Carole retorted. "When I visited Green Grove eleven years ago everyone had nice houses and cars, television sets and indoor plumbing. They all wore shoes. I expect Dad exaggerated to amuse you."

"Maybe," Marsha Coldren admitted. "He was full of fun. Oh, Carole, I just wish you could have known him."

"So do I," Carole said softly, thinking of the father who had died when she was two.

Curiosity about his side of the family, whose name she bore, had always been keen in Carole. That was why, at seventeen, she had leaped at the chance to visit her "mountain relatives." Her continuing curiosity explained why she had now accepted an assignment to go back to Green Grove and interview feisty, ninety-year-old Aunt Eugenia Coldren Goodwin, a living repository of old legends and stories about the Coldrens. Aunt Eugenia was one of the last witnesses to the final explosion of the long-time feud between the Coldrens and a neighboring family for whom they had scant regard. The final shoot-out, from the banks of the Hilamunga River on April 10, 1899, had left twenty-one people dead. Aunt Eugenia had been only seven years old at the time, but, according to Carole's cousin, Susan Coldren Briggs, the memories were as fresh in her mind as yesterday's. Indeed, fresher, since Aunt Eugenia sometimes tended to drift off and forget exactly what had happened yesterday.

"Auntie has always refused to talk to nosy reporters, folklore specialists or even historians," Susan had written to Carole. "But since you're a Coldren as well as a writer, she's willing to talk to you. Please consider coming!"

Not only did Carole consider the offer, she leaped at it. Susan's letter had arrived when Carole was providentially between jobs, and although she wondered whether her slick copywriting talents, which paid so well in Houston, were equal to the task, her own desire to know the Coldren family history was too great a lure to deny. Furthermore, a Dr. Thomas Kaufman of Wimberly College in North Carolina wanted to publish the resulting volume and had agreed to pay Carole at her usual rate.

So here she was now, stranded and stuck a scant twenty miles from the home of her fore-bearers.

Carole managed to raise the hood of the car without mishap and poked around in its unfamiliar innards, looking for something obviously disconnected or sizzling, but everything appeared to be in maddeningly good order. Next, she bent down and peered beneath the car. Nothing dangled loose or dripped from its underside, either.

Angrily, Carole kicked a tire, then tied a white handkerchief on her radio antenna and settled down to await someone's response to this distress signal. But it was noon, and traffic along the blacktopped highway was scanty. A couple of cars whizzed past without deigning to stop. Finally, a pickup truck that looked in far worse shape than Carole's car clattered off the road.

When Carole saw the Good Samaritan crawling out she smiled grimly, thinking how her mother would enjoy the sight of a real, live hillbilly.

At least the elderly man in overalls, with a plug of tobacco stuck in his jaw, was shod and kindly. After allowing that he didn't know "a dern thing about cars 'cept they're contrary," he offered to send back assistance from a garage in Green Grove. Carole expressed her appreciation, wondering privately if he would ever reach the town when he went rattling off again, chickens clucking in the back of his truck.

At last, after waiting another hour, Carole saw a white tow truck winding along the road which came from the direction of Green Grove. She straightened up from the fender and silently blessed the conscientious old hillbilly. Then the two truck came into view, its name emblazoned in bright, bold red letters: *Haughton Towing & Wrecker Service.*

"Oh, no," Carole murmured with a sinking feeling in the pit of her stomach.

On April 10, 1899, across a narrow river where hot guns had blazed in a classic mountain feud, ten Coldrens and eleven Haughtons had died. The guns were stilled now and several new generations of each family had been born since that dark and tragic day. Gradually, civilization and culture had come to the mountain people. But memories in these hills were long. Ancient grudges continued to be remembered and rehashed. Rivalries between the clans continued to run strong.

Susan's last letter to Carole had touched fleetingly on the Haughtons. "They own most of the automobile agencies and garages in town, so we have to deal with them. They're certainly continuing their long tradition of larceny, I might add!"

Tactfully, Susan had written no more. No doubt she remembered that eleven years ago young Jon Haughton—the nickname was short, of course, for Jonathan—a dark and dashing civil engineer, had stolen more than kisses from Carole Coldren. Indeed, for a brief, bittersweet time, he had robbed her of all reason and logic.

Occasionally, in her more fanciful moments over the last decade, Carole had wondered if Jon Haughton had captured her heart for all time. Twice Carole had come close to marrying someone else. Twice the memory of a mountain man's burning kisses and warm, tenderly roving hands had forced her to realize that the affection she felt for each of her fiancés was simply not love.

Face it, Carole, a wise little voice whispered in her head, *one reason you've come back is because you've never been able to forget him.*

He's probably off in some godforsaken place building a hydroelectric plant or whatever! she answered the inner voice cynically. *I came back to rid myself of those overromanticized, unrealistic memories.*

The tow truck stopped and a young man leaped out. He looked about eighteen, possibly younger, and unmistakably like a Haughton. Tall and lithe, he strolled toward Carole. Like any teenager who worked in a garage, he wore faded jeans and a grease-smeared T-shirt. "What's wrong, lady?" he called cheerfully.

"I don't know," Carole said, her own voice terse.

His gaze rested on her for a moment, half-shyly, half-admiringly. It was the look a boy sends to an attractive "older woman." Then he began inspecting the car much as Carole had done—raising the hood, peering beneath it, and trying the ignition switch.

"Can't tell what it is out here in the wild-woods," he said blithely. "We'll have to haul it into town."

That's probably going to cost me a bundle, Carole thought dismally, remembering Susan's line about the Haughtons' "larceny."

The boy stood waiting, looking at her tentatively. Carole pushed back a lock of her thick red-blond hair, and his eyes followed the gesture. Fleetingly she wondered if he'd recognize her as one of the enemy clan. She had the coloring of the Scotch-English Coldrens—big brown eyes, creamy skin and, of course, that telltale hair.

"All right," Carole sighed, "tow it in."

With a great clanking of chains and grinding of gears, the young Haughton boy attached Carole's car to the tow truck. Then he ran around and gallantly opened the cab door on the passenger side for Carole. At least the kid has nice manners, Carole conceded, climbing up and into the truck.

Jon Haughton had always had nice manners, too. . . .

To stop the flow of unwelcome thoughts, Carole turned to the boy who slid beneath the steering wheel. "What's your name?" she asked him.

"I'm Terry. Terry Rodgers."

"You're not a Haughton?" she said, startled.

He glanced at her and his slow smile made memories chime. "My mother was. Sally Haughton was her name."

"Oh." Blindly Carole stared out the window, no longer seeing the blue-hazed mountains or the meadow of wildflowers. During that long-ago summer Jon had often mentioned his older sister Sally. This boy was his nephew.

"What's your name, ma'am?" Terry asked engagingly.

"Carole Coldren," she said, and curiously awaited his reaction.

Immediately both his hands flew up in the air. "Please don't shoot," he said mildly.

Carole was so surprised that she burst out laughing, and Terry chimed in with a low chuckle. Oh, what a ridiculous situation this was, she thought, both charmed and amused by the boy's sense of humor.

"Put your hands down, Terry, and let's get rolling," Carole said when she had stopped laughing.

"O.K." Cheerfully he complied and they rumbled off. After a moment he darted another glance at Carole. "You know, I kinda thought you looked like a Coldren when I first saw you, but your license plate says Texas."

"I grew up there, so I'm not part of the local feud," she informed him.

"Not much of a feud anymore," he said. "Oh, some of the old folks still kick and holler and carry on, but I like most of the Coldrens well

14

enough—except maybe for Blake. He's a bully in anybody's town."

"And just who is the Haughtons' bully?" Carole said, half-teasingly.

"Oh, that would be Lon." Terry touched his forehead. "'Course he's not too smart, so you shouldn't hold it against him."

"I'll remember," said Carole.

"There's a Coldren girl a year behind me in school who's mighty nice," Terry went on. "Betsy is her name."

Betsy was Susan's younger sister. "She's my first cousin," Carole told him.

"She sure is pretty," Terry said wistfully. "Friendly, too. I used to wish—" His voice stopped abruptly.

He wished he could ask Betsy for a date, Carole realized. Her eyes narrowing, she glanced again at Terry. He seemed like a nice enough kid, but she didn't want young Betsy hurt by a Haughton as she herself had been.

"You back here visiting relatives?" Terry asked Carole.

"Yes. It's only my second visit." Inside Carole the nagging, knowing voice whispered, Go ahead and ask him. Get it over with! "I visited here for the entire summer eleven years ago," Carole added. "I met several of your family then. Jon is the one I remember best."

"He's my uncle," the boy confirmed. From his casual tone Carole knew that Terry had never heard anything about her and Jon. Undoubtedly both families had squelched all talk of that summer romance.

"Where is Jon now?" Carole asked, her voice casual. The last time she'd had news of him, from Susan, he'd been involved in a water recovery project in the Far East.

"Why, he's here," Terry answered.

"Here! In Green Grove?" Absolute shock left Carole immobile while her heart lurched and thundered.

"He came back a couple of months ago. He's in charge of building a big earth dam below the falls of the Hilamunga River. It's going to take four or five years." Pride rang in Terry's young voice.

"I see," said Carole, staring down at her hands.

"I sure hope I can help Uncle Jon build that dam," Terry went on enthusiastically. "I want to be an engineer myself someday."

The kid had a classic case of hero worship, Carole realized numbly. Then she carefully framed her next question. "I guess Jon's family has moved back here with him?"

"Oh, he's not married."

"He's not?" Gratefully Carole received this fascinating bit of information.

"No. Seems like he was engaged to some girl a few years after he finished college, but she died."

"Oh." Jon had just obtained his master's degree the summer when Carole met him.

"Yeah, I've heard he was really crazy about

that girl. 'Course, he's dated lots of women since then, but Mom's about to give up on his ever getting hitched."

Carole looked blindly through the windshield. So Jon had finally met his own true love only to lose her. She wondered why she felt such savage pleasure that someone had finally caused him suffering, too.

"You mind if I play the radio?" Terry asked.

"No," Carole replied tonelessly. Immediately she felt ashamed of her hostile reaction toward Jon and distressed that after so many years she still responded that way.

She listened to a station playing bluegrass music during the rest of the drive into town. On the outskirts of Green Grove, as red-brick buildings and houses appeared, Terry jerked a thumb toward the right. "Here we are, Miss Coldren. Garage and wrecking yard."

She looked toward a large barnlike building. Like the wrecker it was painted in pristine white with the Haughton name emblazoned in red.

The truck turned in, Carole's car squeaking in protest behind them. She turned in her seat to regard it anxiously and saw that another car was also pulling in behind the tow truck. This was a low sleek car in steel gray, and sunlight glittered off its highly waxed roof.

Terry's brakes gave a protesting grind when he stopped the wrecker in front of the white and red building. He threw a casual glance into the rearview mirror, then gave a low whistle. "Speak of the devil—"

"What?" Carole said.

"You just asked me about Uncle Jon and here he is. That's his new Porsche 944 right behind us."

Carole had less than a moment to brace herself. Her mind reeled crazily, and she was stunned by the strange sequence of events. Imagine Jon Haughton being the third person she met on entering Grove County! A thousand times in her mind she had visualized a future meeting with him, but never, never was it to happen like this. Not when she was road-weary and her car disabled, leaving her virtually at the mercy of the Haughtons. No, Carole had always intended to be her most cool, poised self if she ever saw Jon again. Instead her heart churned like a giddy teenager's, her mouth was dry as cotton, while her fingernails dug into palms gone wet.

All those thoughts raced through her mind in a twinkling while Terry leaped down from the tow truck and ran around to open the door for Carole.

Shakily she got out of the truck and deliberately turned her back toward the sleek oncoming car. I'm afraid to look, afraid to see him! Oh, God, he's bound to have changed!

"Hey, Terry, what are you dragging in today?"

The voice aimed in their direction was low with a slight drawl. It was the exact same voice that Carole had heard for years in her dreams.

"Lady's car broke down, Uncle Jon," Terry

called back. "Just picked her up out at Posy Meadow. She says she knows you."

"Always glad when my friends are rescued." Brisk steps crunched on the gravel behind Carole.

She could no longer avoid facing him Carole knew. Her hands clenched even more tightly and her head went up. She swung around and her eyes collided with Jon Haughton's.

What crossed her face in that moment of recognition Carole didn't know, but Jon stopped abruptly and she heard him suck in his breath.

"Hello, Jon," Carole said quietly. Mercifully, her voice didn't quaver. It was bad enough that the blood pounded through her veins at sight of him, her heart rhythm went berserk, and there was an awful, ominous roaring in her ears.

From his stance and his shocked black eyes, Carole could see that he was utterly dumb-struck.

At least she'd had that one single moment in which to compose herself, but—oh, he wasn't supposed to still look like this! Had he changed at all, this splendid man of thirty-five who now wore an expensive wheat-colored suit instead of the jeans or khakis she remembered?

Yes, of course, he was unmistakably older, but the years had only added to his attractiveness. Faint lines lay crinkled around the corners of his piercing eyes, and a few hairs at his temples were lightly silvered. Years before he had been quite lean, still carrying traces of a boy's rangy

thinness, but now his always magnificent physique had filled out by at least twenty pounds.
She had forgotten how his six-feet-plus towered
over her, had forgotten, too, some of the exqui-
sitely molded lines and planes of his face.

She hadn't forgotten the touch of his crisp
black hair, as thick as ever, nor had she forgotten his proud straight nose and long, full lips.
Now, though, his mouth was compressed in
astonishment or shock.

Carole knew she must seize the offensive
while she still could, although the muscles
around her own mouth felt too stiff and painful
to move.

"You're looking well," she managed. "It's
been a long time."

"Carole Coldren." Jon spoke her name like a
man in a trance. Then, before her wondering
eyes, Carole watched him pull himself together.
His thick jet-black eyebrows drew in toward the
bridge of his nose, and the dark eyes beneath
them narrowed. He smiled almost mockingly,
she thought, although when he spoke his voice
was quiet and courteous.

"You're quite right, it has been a long time.
What brings you back to the mountains, Carole?
It was my impression that you were quite glad to
get away."

That was because you dropped me like a hot
potato! Carole thought, and even across the
distance of eleven years the thought stung her to
anger.

Aloud she said coldly, "I've always loved the mountains. It was some of the people here I didn't love or admire."

Catty. Tasteless. Tacky. Carole knew she was being all three, yet she seemed powerless to stop herself.

"Certainly you made your feelings on that score most apparent," said Jon, his voice gone cool and remote.

"Hey, you guys—" As Terry's perplexed voice intruded on their conversation, both Carole and Jon turned toward the boy. In the surprise of her reunion with Jon, Carole had actually forgotten that the kid was standing there.

"I thought you two would be *glad* to see each other," Terry said hesitantly.

"Oh, don't mind us." Swiftly Jon clapped a hand on his nephew's shoulder. "Carole and I always struck sparks off each other. It never meant anything, did it, Carole?"

His cynical words hit her with the impact of a blow. Once the sparks they struck had meant everything to Carole, though not to him. "Of course not," she agreed, for Terry's sake.

When Terry continued to look at them dubiously, Jon quickly took charge. "Pull Miss Coldren's car around back and get one of the mechanics on it pronto. I'm sure she doesn't want to be delayed any longer than necessary."

Terry looked relieved. He bounded back toward the wrecker, and after a moment it clattered away.

"Is it still 'Miss Coldren'?" Jon asked, regarding Carole with a burning gaze that she couldn't begin to fathom.

Carole drew a breath, trying to regain her own equilibrium. "Yes, it still is."

"You mean you *never* married? That's quite remarkable." Jon spoke smoothly, but his rapid breathing betrayed him. Of course, her own heart was pounding but what had disturbed Jon so? Was he angry?

He confirmed her suspicion by adding, "Or have you left a string of ex-husbands behind you, like your cousin Wynne?"

"As a matter of fact, I've devoted myself to my career," she replied in an ice-glazed voice.

"You look like you've been successful at it." Jon's eyes narrowed, but his voice had again become courteous.

"I have. You look like you've done quite well yourself, Jon." Be nice now, the voice in her head urged.

"Yes. Somehow I've managed in spite of being 'haughty as a Haughton.'"

The ancient phrase dated from the Coldrens' and Haughtons' bloody feud. Once Carole and Jon had teased each other with such quaint old words. "Since I'm a career woman, you're bound to think I'm 'cold-hearted as a Coldren,'" she replied lightly.

"You don't look it." Jon's hands went to his narrow hips while his dark eyes continued to survey her. "But why are we standing out here in the sun? I'm sure you'd like to get your car attended to."

"Yes," Carole admitted, and although her voice had finally failed her and quavered audibly, it held dignity, too. "I'd also like the opportunity to freshen up and grab a bite to eat, if you'll direct me to a cafe. It's been a long time since breakfast."

"That's all quite easy to arrange," said Jon. "Just follow me." He started toward the white barnlike building with such long strides that Carole found it difficult to keep pace with him.

Jon flew up three steps, then stopped to open the door for Carole. When she moved toward him their eyes met again. His looked storm-whipped, with something unreadable flickering in their dark depths. Unaccountably Carole's heart lurched again, and at that exact moment, her foot tripped over the door sill.

"Careful!" Jon's hand shot out to grip her elbow. Even through her clothes Carole could feel the firm, warm pressure of his touch, and her entire body was suddenly electrified. She began tingling, feeling eager and vitally alive.

Jon's hand dropped away, and Carole despised herself for responding to his touch. "Thank you," she whispered, and preceded him into the office of the garage.

When cool, refreshing air-conditioning hit her face Carole's knees sagged and began to tremble. She felt overcome by her unsettled emotions and reaction to the meeting with Jon. Abruptly and unbidden came the memory of his very first kiss. It had been the Fourth of July and all the young people in the mountains had congregated on the banks of the Hilamunga River.

Alone there, in a grove dense with green trees, Jon Haughton had leaned over and brushed Carole's lips with his own warm ones. Even that brief a touch had ignited small fires inside her, and for the first time in her life, Carole had hurled herself into a man's arms. . . .

"Carole, this is my brother Robert. He owns the garage." Carole came back to awareness of the present as Jon introduced her to another lean, darkly handsome man.

"If you'll just sign the service ticket, Miss Coldren, we'll get on your car right away." Robert Haughton's manner was pleasant, but strictly businesslike. In his early forties, he was obviously a busy man.

Carole signed automatically where he indicated, and Robert handed the ticket to a rangy long-haired girl who worked behind the counter. Another Haughton, Carole thought with recognition, realizing wryly that she was certainly in the heart of the enemy's camp.

"This is my niece, Lila," Jon continued the introductions smoothly. "Lila, Miss Coldren has been standing in the hot sun for a long time. Would you show her to the water fountain and the restroom?"

The lithe girl, who was probably around twenty, came from behind the counter and regarded

Carole not unsympathetically. "The ladies' room is this way," she said.

Carole followed her down the hall, noticing that Lila wore a rose-colored shirt with a designer label tucked into a pair of name-brand jeans. Some hillbillies! she thought, smiling faintly.

Lila opened a door and flipped on a light switch. "Call me if you need anything," she said helpfully.

At least the younger generation of Haughtons acted friendly, Carole reflected as she bathed her flushed face in a stream of icy cold water.

She found sweet-smelling soap and a soft hand towel, then looked around curiously. This was a cheerful little bathroom with ivy design wallpaper and a large clear mirror that ran half the length of the room.

Thoughtfully, Carole turned back to the mirror and studied her own reflection. Jon seemed so untouched by time, so utterly unchanged, except for that flash of cynicism and the strange something flickering in the depths of his eyes.

Had time been less kind to her? Truthfully, Carole didn't think so. Of course, she was twenty-eight now, but her waist still measured the same as it had when she was seventeen, and she possessed all the right womanly curves in just the right proportions. Her stomach retained the flatness of youth, while her legs were long and shapely. Beneath her white pullover was a firm bosom with natural uplift that no woman need be ashamed of. Because she was tall—

almost five-seven—she looked equally good dressed in skirts or pants.

Satisfied with the scrutiny of her figure, Carole studied her face next. But no matter how closely she peered into the mirror she could detect no signs of aging there. She didn't even have the crinkling laugh lines by her eyes that were so devastatingly attractive on Jon.

Her oval-shaped face, wide forehead and good bone structure continued to enhance her nearly flawless skin. Her mouth was well formed and coral colored, her nose straight, her chin line firm. Her brown eyes were absolutely great, she admitted frankly, large and slightly tip-tilted at the far corners with a thick sweep of long curly lashes.

Rapidly Carole stroked blusher onto her cheekbones, touched her lips with gloss and smoothed down one unruly red-brown eyebrow, darker by several shades than her hair. She cast a final, firm look into her eyes and thought, Steady, girl. You may be about to get shafted again by the Haughtons, this time over a garage bill!

Alert and wary, she went back out to face them and found that Jon awaited her.

His eyes skimmed her rapidly from her thick, just-brushed hair to the fresh touches of makeup she'd applied. Then his gaze dropped, raking her from her neck to her feet and back up again. Carole felt herself flushing, feeling as though Jon were mentally disrobing her. His eyes lingered on her breasts until she felt he could see the smooth pale skin beneath her lacy bra.

"Is my appearance satisfactory?" she said coolly. His gaze affected her like a physical touch, and her body warmed with awareness.

"Very. I'm surprised you're still allowed to run loose. Don't they have real men in Texas anymore?"

"Of course," she said with a toss of her head. "I'm just quite selective."

"That I don't doubt for a moment!"

Carole didn't like the thrust of this conversation or being the object of such an intense scrutiny. She turned to walk into the waiting room, but Jon's voice stopped her. "Why so worried, Carole?"

So he had detected her reaction. "I'm just anxious about my car," she replied, for that, at least, was true.

"Relax. Robert says it's still under warranty."

"What about the towing charge?" Carole asked.

"That will probably be substantial," he admitted, "but I'm sure a car as new as yours has adequate insurance coverage—"

"Of course," she cut in.

"Well, the usual policy carries a provision for towing charges. If you'll give Lila your insurance card, I'll ask her to get on the phone and verify that for you," Jon offered.

"You mean I might not have to pay all the towing charges?" Carole inquired.

"I don't think you'll have to pay any of them," he said firmly.

Carole produced her card, and Jon carried it to

Lila, who reached immediately for her telephone.

"See? Few problems are truly insoluble," Jon said when he returned to Carole's side. "Ready to go?"

"Thank you," Carole said grudgingly, but with relief. Then the impact of his last words sank in. "Go? Where are we going?"

"Why, for lunch, of course. You said you hadn't eaten, and by coincidence, neither have I."

"You don't have to—I mean, I scarcely expect—" Carole began to stammer.

He cupped her elbow in warm tingly fingers. "Come on," he insisted with a smile. "No protests are permitted."

Chapter Two

*W*hat am I doing in this car, alone again with Jon Haughton? Carole wondered as he deftly guided his gleaming Porsche up and down hill through the winding city streets. The calm she'd been able to impose on her emotions had deserted her once again. In the confines of the small car his nearness and physical attractiveness seemed overwhelming.

Carole turned in the leather bucket seat to dart a quick glance at Jon. His black hair sprang from his high forehead with life and vitality, and the lines of his jaw and throat were strong, clean-cut. Beneath his lightly tanned brow his eyebrows soared like black wings. Stubby but thick eyelashes concealed his black eyes.

His hard trim body was relaxed, and he drove seemingly without effort. Carole had forgotten the way he always merged himself with an automobile so that shifts, stops and curves were taken smoothly.

Clean masculine smells surrounded Jon—spicy soap, shampoo and a dash of aftershave mingled with his own healthy fragrance. When he turned his head to speak to her, his breath was warm and sweetly exhilarating.

"The town hasn't changed much," he remarked. "Fortunately we lie off the beaten track, so we're bypassed by the hordes of tourists who pour into North Carolina.

"That's a blessing," Carole concurred, thinking of Houston's rampant and almost uncontrolled growth in recent years.

"The restaurants haven't changed, either," he went on. "The Cabin is still the best in town. That's where we're going."

"Oh," said Carole noncommittally. She drew a ragged breath, wondering why his presence continued to disturb her so.

Jon braked for a stop sign, then glanced to his left, where a police car sat parked beneath a flowering dogwood tree. "Well, well," he murmured, "the gendarmes are out to nail speedsters and stop-sign runners."

Carole's gaze followed his. "So they are."

"You'll be reassured to know that the Coldrens still run the sheriff's office. If you feel unsafe with me, Carole—and from the way you're squirming about on your seat, I'm afraid you do—you can roll down the car window and yell."

Nettled, she threw him a scathing look. "I'm not afraid of you, Jon Haughton!"

"Oh, you're not any longer? Perhaps you've grown up, after all."

"What do you mean by that?" Carole said, stung.

"Why, I was once led to believe that I scared

the daylights out of you." Jon's voice was barbed.

"I don't know what you're talking about, Jon," Carole whispered and wished her pulses would quit racing so.

He threw her an inscrutable look. "I doubt that," he said softly. "I very much doubt that." He slid the car into gear, and they glided past the stop sign.

Carole's confusion deepened. Broderick "Buck" Coldren, one of her father's brothers, had been sheriff of Grove County eleven years ago and obviously still was. "Do you mean Uncle Buck once talked to you about me or—" She stopped, unable to say more in the dawn of an awful suspicion.

"We had a thirty-second *conversation*," said Jon, putting heavy emphasis on the word. "However, his advice was sound. In retrospect, I learned to appreciate it. Now that I'm back in Green Grove, Buck and I both tip our hats to one another and get along swell. I do think bygones should be bygones, don't you?"

His double meaning did not escape her. "Right now, I don't know what I think," Carole said, turning again to look out her window.

Exactly what was Jon carefully neglecting to reveal? What could be said in a thirty-second conversation? Uncle Buck was not a subtle man. Had he roared, "Stay away from my niece!" and had Jon replied meekly, "Yes, sir"? Was he the kind of groveling coward who toadied to authority?

Carole found that difficult, almost impossible to believe. While she had been quite young eleven years ago, Jon had been a man of twenty-four, a college graduate with two degrees who was working on his first engineering job, a bridge being built seventy-five miles from Green Grove. Could a small-town sheriff scare such a man away? It didn't seem logical.

But something had certainly happened to end their romance. Carole thought again of those agonizing weeks in late August that she'd once endured, wondering why Jon didn't call her or seek her out. Had he lost all respect for her? Had he lost all interest? Had he found someone else? Left town? She had never known and she still didn't.

She swung back to confront him, questions bubbling on her lips, and saw that he was pulling into The Cabin's parking lot. His face, in profile, looked so cool and forbidding that the words died on Carole's lips. Perhaps he would say more at lunch. If not, then she would simply enjoy dining at his expense. After all she had suffered for him once, Jon Haughton owed her that much!

The Cabin was exactly what its name suggested, a large, authentic log cabin that had been restored and turned into a restaurant. Although its exterior capitalized on the area's mountain heritage, inside it was modern, air-conditioned, and featured an international cuisine. Jon guided Carole to a table by the huge old chimney. A red-checkered tablecloth and a white candle in a night-stand candleholder decorated each table. Jon struck a match and lit their candle, then took menus from the waitress who had rushed over.

"If you want to go native, they serve venison roast and rabbit stew, but, frankly, I much prefer their lasagna," he suggested.

"I'll try it," said Carole, "because I'm not fond of mountain cooking, either, although I do remember yummy dumplings, biscuits and spoon bread."

She ordered lasagna, a salad and iced tea. Jon's order duplicated hers except that he asked for coffee. Their salads arrived immediately, and Carole attacked hers hungrily.

From across the room a stocky man stood up and waved in their direction. Immediately Jon lifted his napkin out of his lap and dropped it beside his plate. "Excuse me a moment, Carole. There's a fellow engineer over there I dare not ignore."

Did you also rush to do Uncle Buck's bidding? Carole wondered, but she nodded without comment.

She watched Jon stride across the room, moving with his smooth easy gait, and despite what she suspected now, something about him still turned a knife in her heart. For a moment it hurt to eat, to breathe, to move.

She remembered her first glimpse of him on that long-ago Fourth of July. Not that she'd known she would meet any of the Haughtons, of course. All Carole knew was that she, Susan, and little pig-tailed Betsy were going to a picnic on the banks of the river. Susan's new boy-friend, Reggie Briggs, would pick them up in his truck, and at the picnic grounds they would join several other cousins that Carole had already met.

"Jean and Connie will be watching for us," Susan said, her busy fingers flying as she and Carole packed the two picnic hampers. "Wynne, too," she added, after a moment.

"Oh, not that catty Wynne!" Carole wailed.

She had also met Wynne Coldren, Uncle Buck's daughter, and liked her not at all. Although Wynne was the family beauty, with long auburn hair and grass-green eyes, she had a manner as imperious as Aunt Eugenia's and she was used to getting her own way.

Carole especially disliked Wynne's manner of ordering Susan about. "Why do you put up with Wynne?" she asked Susan while they packed their lunch.

Her cousin's fresh yet rather plain face took on a pinched look. "Because I want her to leave Reggie and me alone," Susan said painfully. "Wynne's so pretty she can always get any guy she goes after. A year ago, when I was dating another boy, I crossed Wynne and we had a blazing argument. By Monday she had my boy-friend." A sigh escaped Susan. "Since then, especially since Reggie moved to town, I leave Wynne alone!"

"Oh, surely not all the boys in Grove County fall at her feet?" Carole said disbelievingly.

"Yes, they do," Susan retorted. Then, after a moment, she said, "Well, there's one guy who didn't, but he hardly counts, anyway. He's a Haughton!"

"Oh." Despite herself, Carole smiled. At that time she'd regarded the two families' enmity as amusing and eccentric, although the fact that dating between them was taboo carried rather ominous overtones.

"Yes, Jon Haughton wouldn't have anything to do with Wynne." Susan related the tale with relish. "Of course, that's not surprising. Even though Wynne's gorgeous and he's a good-looking devil, the Haughtons draw the line at Coldrens the same as we do with them. Wynne was crazy to ever get interested in Jon. If Uncle Buck had found out, he would have locked her up for a hundred years!"

Armed with this interesting bit of information, Carole went off to the picnic. It was thronged with young people who had brought kegs of beer, cold watermelons, transistor radios and cameras. There was swimming and baseball, laughter and horseplay.

The boys soon drifted away to play ball, while the girls visited with friends. Then they located a picnic table and spread out fried chicken, potato salad and cole slaw. Since the guys had not returned, the girls went in search of them, passing a number of other groups along the way.

Carole, gazing around elatedly at everything

and everyone, felt a sudden sharp pinch on her arm. "Don't look at those men on the right," Wynne said loudly into Carole's ear.

"Why?" said Carole, annoyed by her bossy cousin's clutch.

"Because they're Haughtons, that's why, and that stuck-up Jon Haughton is looking straight at you!"

Slowly and deliberately, Carole stopped. She turned and looked in the forbidden direction at the forbidden men, and her eyes skimmed a group of lean dark faces, intent on their own conversation. Then she saw the last man. As tall and lean as the others, but far more handsome, he wore khakis, his short-sleeved shirt open at the throat. His reckless black eyes looked straight into hers, frankly and appraisingly, yet without a trace of hostility.

"Don't look at him, I told you, Carole Coldren!" Wynne practically screamed.

A smile tugged at the corners of Jon Haughton's firm, full lips and started across his face. Though Carole could see that he was a grown man, he flashed her a mischievous boy's delighted smile, an irresistible smile, as he waited to see just what she would do next.

Carole smiled back. Just watch me, she communicated to him.

"Carole, don't you dare smile at that—that—" Words failed Wynne, but her fury was so intense that she pinched Carole even more sharply than before.

Carole turned calmly to her cousin, whose

face was not beautiful now but ugly and contorted in her rage. "Go butt a stump, Wynne!" she said, her voice implacable.

At Carole's remark, Jon Haughton threw back his dark head and roared with laughter. Wynne flushed scarlet while Susan, Betsy, Connie and Jean all exchanged horrified looks. They hurried away and, after a moment, Wynne rushed after them. Leisurely, Carole brought up the rear.

She didn't look back, but she could feel Jon Haughton's gaze sweeping from the crown of her head to the soles of her feet. A warm rush of feeling told her so.

Lunch for the Coldrens was subdued. Wynne sulked and refused to eat. Susan, Connie and Jean each made several leading remarks, all designed to enlighten their city cousin about the Haughtons. The whole family was untrustworthy, no-account and generally lower than a snake's belly, Carole heard with disbelief. The Coldren boys, who could have cared less about some old feud, bolted their food and dashed back to resume their ballgame.

After lunch, when the girls were eager to walk down to the mill house, Carole offered to remain behind and put away the leftovers. She was tired of Wynne's sulks and the others' well-meaning lectures against the Haughtons. After they had left, she was quite content to be alone.

Carole had just closed the second of the two picnic hampers when she knew she was no longer alone. The hair prickled on the back of her neck, and she felt warmth flood her body as though she were being held and caressed. She knew it was *him*.

"Hello, Carole Coldren," he said quietly.

"Hello, Jon Haughton," she returned over her shoulder.

He walked to her side, she set down the basket, and they looked searchingly at one another. She memorized his face in that moment. Then, simultaneously, they burst out laughing in remembrance of her earlier defiance of Wynne and from the simple, joyous exuberance of having discovered each other as well. . . .

That was the way it had begun between them more than a decade ago, but Carole still remembered each detail as though it had been burned on her brain.

Abruptly she returned to realization of her present surroundings. She saw Jon threading his way back through the tables, and again, the sheer sight of him made the breath catch in her throat.

Painfully Carole faced an unwelcome truth. She had thought she was back in Green Grove to investigate and write about the Coldrens' and Haughtons' feud. Of course, that subject did interest her . . . but not as much as the tall man coming toward her who represented, in a purely personal way, the last installment of that feud.

Jon gave her a brief smile of apology as he dropped down into his seat. She waited to see what, if anything, he'd say, but their waitress reappeared promptly bearing plates of steaming lasagna, and Jon waived conversation in favor of food. He ate quickly, neatly and was soon finished. Carole, determined not to delay him, took a final mouthful of the delicious tomato-smothered pasta, then indicated, with a nod, that she was ready to go.

Jon paid the bill, and they were soon back in his Porsche, whizzing across town. "Your car should be ready by now," he remarked. "I'm sure you're eager to be on your way."

"My relatives probably wonder what's happened to me," Carole said wryly.

Abruptly Jon braked his car, although they were in the midst of a quiet, tree-lined street. Red brick houses, framed with flowering shrubs and set back from the street, were the only signs of life.

"Why are we stopping here?" Carole asked, bewildered.

Almost before she knew what was happening, John had gripped her chin with hard relentless fingers. His face moved downward, and before Carole could say another word, his lips captured and possessed hers.

This was not a tender, passionate kiss, like those she had been unable to forget. Those same lips could be as hard as his hands, and now they applied pressure almost cruelly to the softness of Carole's mouth. Yet despite her indignation at being seized by him and kissed so unlovingly, a part of Carole still responded to Jon. Fires, ignited by his lips, leaped to life and burned in her chest, her spine, running like molten liquid down her arms and legs.

Though his mouth still imprisoned hers, the kiss deepening even more, Jon's hands dropped to Carole's breasts. One firm hand confidently cupped a soft mound while the other stroked its mate. His thumb flicked inquiringly over her nipple, and it hardened immediately under his warm touch.

Desperately Carole sought to break the embrace, but she was unable to move, much less struggle. How could her body turn traitor when her mind resented this so? How terrible to feel such a wave of longing and raw hunger, yet Carole felt her whole body trembling and throbbing with reawakened desire.

As abruptly as Jon had seized her, he let her go. "Just what was that all about?" Carole asked through lips that felt bruised. Although her breasts heaved with the effort to control her feelings, her voice at least emerged cool and sophisticated.

"Just checking out old sparks," Jon said, his words uneven. He turned back to the steering wheel, and the car jerked ahead without his customary driving smoothness.

A thousand questions flooded Carole's mind as she huddled against her side of the automobile, but she didn't even know where or how to begin. The sight of Jon's brooding visage offered no clues.

His voice had sounded bitter. His kiss and touch had been hurtful, almost as though he longed to punish her by arousing her. But what on earth did *he* have to be bitter about when she—Carole—had always been the party so grievously wronged?

She had been a virgin he charmed, seduced and dumped!

Jon drew his car up before the large white garage, then leaned across Carole's shrinking body to open her door.

"I see your compact parked outside. That means work on it is finished." His voice sounded remote, and his glance at her appeared indifferent. "Don't worry, Carole Coldren, I won't bother you again."

Carole clambered out of the car, since that was obviously what Jon wanted her to do. She slammed the door, and once again his car started forward jerkily. Swiftly Jon drove away, leaving Carole staring, mystified, after him.

Jon Haughton can go to hell!

Although Carole didn't say the words aloud, they ran furiously through her head a half-dozen times while her emotions boiled and seethed like a caldron.

She stomped into the garage and demanded her bill. Robert Haughton produced it, explaining what had been wrong with her car, but Carole was too upset to comprehend his dry recital of machinery failure.

The charge was nominal. Ten dollars for paperwork and the phone call. At least Carole hadn't been taken to the cleaners by this particular set of Haughtons, but the thought brought her no cheer. Neither did Lila's sly inquiry about whether she'd enjoyed her lunch.

"Yes, indeed," Carole said shortly.

"Uncle Jon owes us one." The girl smiled, producing Carole's car keys. "We'd all planned to have lunch together, but that was before he saw you."

Carole made a terse reply and fled back out to her car.

It started easily, settling into its customary purr. "You'd better behave from now on," Carole warned her automobile, "or I'll leave you to rust next time. I don't need any more encounters with the haughty Haughtons!"

At least her sense of humor was asserting itself, along with a perspective of sorts. She had been back in Green Grove less than three hours and already Jon Haughton had rejected her once again!

The town hadn't changed much, Jon had said, and for the most part Carole found his words to be true. Green Grove sprawled over hilltops, its streets winding up and down. While certain teenage hangouts were gone and new ones had sprung up, Carole had no difficulty finding her way. She saw the high school building, surrounded by yellow buses, and familiar churches, all with steeples pointing heavenward. There was a big country store she remembered with bright flags flying, a town square with a small bandstand, and City Hall. The latter was built of the familiar red bricks with ivy creeping up and over one side. Oh, but the town looks *good*, Carole thought, a serene beautiful haven overshadowed by the marvelous green-timbered mountains.

Automatically Carole turned up a winding street, and a few minutes later she saw the sign she sought for Poplar Street.

Yes, there were the houses of neighbors, people whom she remembered but dimly, and there was the tall blue spruce tree on the corner up ahead. Then Carole slowed, bewildered by all the cars that crowded the street. Her heart skipped when she saw a sheriff's car parked close to the corner. Had something happened? There were no curious crowds milling about. Instead the focal point appeared to be the cozy, old two-story house belonging to Paul and Louise Coldren, her uncle and his wife, the parents of Susan and Betsy. The brick house, shaded by huge trees, looked exactly as it had eleven years ago.

Prominent in front of the house was a car-long space. Carole pulled into it and stopped, feeling a trifle apprehensive. She was beginning to understand that all the cars and, yes, a couple of pickups, too, represented a reception committee of family members. They awaited *her*.

She got out of her car and looked all around, slowly and nostalgically. The same porch swing moved just a trifle in the breeze. The old mailbox by the door bore the Coldren name. There was Aunt Louise's flower bed, too, bright with mid-May offerings: irises, azaleas, and huge bright red poppies. Marigolds, newly set out, promised to be flourishing by summer.

Carole went swiftly up the walk. When she stepped onto the porch she saw a shadow flit by an open window, and blinked in surprise. Why, it was her old nemesis, Wynne Coldren! No one else in the family had such long rippling auburn hair.

No, she wasn't Wynne Coldren any longer, Carole remembered, both from Susan's letters and Jon's barbed remark. Although Wynne was only a couple of years older than herself, she had gone through three marriages and three divorces. Good heavens, *what* was her last name now? No matter. Susan or someone else would be sure to tell her.

I'll be very nice to Wynne, Carole vowed. With all those matrimonial disasters she can't have had an easy time. Wasn't there something equally bad or even worse that had happened to her brother Blake? An illness of some sort? Oh, yes, she recalled, he had developed severe arthritis.

Although Carole had never liked either Wynne or Blake, she was genuinely sorry for their misfortunes and determined to let bygones be. . . .

Purposefully she stopped her thoughts; they reminded her of the man who'd used that phrase so very recently. Hastily Carole brushed at her clothes, then raised her hand and knocked.

"Here she is!" someone called eagerly from inside the house.

The screen door opened and Carole found herself facing a tall, unfamiliar young woman. The slender and radiantly pretty girl laughed in delight. "Oh, Carole, how wonderful to have you back!"

Her soft smile was the only clue to her identity. "Betsy?" Carole whispered and when the girl nodded, Carole extended her arms, laughing. "Oh, Betsy, you're all grown up! What happened to your pigtails?"

"Mom actually saved them." Betsy's pert nose crinkled as she hugged Carole back.

Then everyone seemed to be surrounding Carole at once. Smiling kinfolk hugged her, patted her shoulder or shook her hand while all of them talked at once.

Uncle Paul and Aunt Louise looked definitely older. Wynne was still beautiful, although there was a hard sheen in her green eyes and a petulant droop to her mouth. The other cousins that Carole remembered best, Connie and Jean, both wore satisfied, long-married expressions and eagerly drew forth husbands and small children to meet their Texas relative.

Carole shook hands with Uncle Buck and her cousin Blake. Uncle Buck wore his familiar sheriff's uniform. He'd lost a little hair and gained a little more paunch, but Blake, limping over on crutches, looked almost as Carole recalled. Although he was thirty by now, he still had a faintly untidy look with straggling reddish hair that crept over his shirt collar. His small eyes were set close to the bridge of his nose, and his body was large and hulking, reminding Carole of Terry Rodgers's description: "A bully in anybody's town." Apparently being stricken by a crippling disease had not mellowed Blake, but Carole felt sympathetic enough to pump his hand and ignore her own instinctive feelings of dislike.

Where were Susan and Reggie? Carole wondered next. Then she saw Reggie striding toward her. He was a big, jovial, brown-skinned man with a round face that would look much the same whether he were twenty or sixty. But what was that strange expression he wore? It seemed half-regret and half-apology. Carole didn't understand it, but before she had time to wonder, she saw the thin woman at his side, almost dwarfed by her large husband.

Susan? Oh, dear God, could this starved-looking woman possibly be her beloved cousin Susan? Why, she looked positively anorexic! Carole was even more startled by Susan than she'd been by Betsy, for one did anticipate that children would grow up. What she hadn't ever expected was that smart, sweet Susan, once so daintily slender, would look like a famine victim. Was she ill? No, her bony face held no tinge of sickness or pallor.

Of course, Susan had known her disappointments, too, for despite the fact that she and Reggie had wanted a large family, their babies had never appeared.

Carole hoped her feelings didn't show as she and Susan embraced, then stepped back to regard each other searchingly.

"Have I changed that much?" Susan said

wryly, and Carole knew she hadn't been successful in hiding her dismay.

"Of course not! We've all changed a bit—" Carole began gamely.

"You haven't, except to get prettier," Reggie said to her gallantly.

"Thanks," she said, throwing him a smile. Then Carole felt her face sober as she glanced around the room at all the cousins surrounded by their families. Even Blake stood beside a dowdy little pigeon of a wife. "I'm the only one who's never married," she realized aloud and, all at once, she felt a pang of loneliness.

Again Carole saw that startling change in Reggie's face. Regret, even apology, swept over his features.

Susan also seemed taken aback by Carole's remark. Sadness flared in her soft brown eyes, but she added sturdily, "Oh, you will, Carole. I just know one day you'll marry, too."

Carole swung around, discomfited by their expressions. It wasn't exactly a tragedy to still be single at twenty-eight. Why did they act like it was? She supposed it was because Susan and Reggie were so happy in their own marriage that they wanted the same sort of bliss for everyone else. Yet had *happiness* blessed Susan with that hungrily ravaged face?

For the first time Carole became aware of a stranger in the room. He was seated a short distance away, watching her intently. When he felt Carole's gaze, he unwound his long body from the chair and rose politely.

"I don't believe I've met the gentleman over there," Carole whispered to Susan.

"Oh, my gosh!" Susan wailed. "I've forgotten to introduce you to Dr. Kaufman!" Linking her arm through Carole's, she led her cousin toward the tall man who was approaching them rapidly.

In the flurry of Susan and Reggie's apologies, Carole and Dr. Thomas Kaufman acknowledged each other with smiles and a handshake.

Once again Carole was surprised by a person's appearance. For some reason she had expected the history professor to be old, someone who whiled away his life studying dusty old books and records. Instead she saw a blond man in his early thirties with a lean, arresting face. His hair was so light as to be almost silver, his eyes were deep blue, and he had an attractive cleft in his chin. The glasses he wore heightened the innate intelligence of his face.

He cut smoothly through Susan's torrent of words. "Don't worry about a thing," he assured her. "I was enjoying the sight of the reunion with Carole."

"What do you think of our writer?" Susan said proudly, thrusting Carole forward. Then she took a discreet step back. "I know you two have so many things you want to discuss."

"Yes. I look forward to that, Dr. Kaufman," Carole said, realizing that the pressure of the man's hand on hers was quite pleasant.

"I can tell that the greater pleasure will be mine." He smiled.

At first Carole thought he had simply voiced a polite sentiment, then she saw the lively interest in his eyes. Was he appreciating her as a writer, a woman—or both? After Jon's put-down she felt herself warmed by his obvious admiration.

"Refreshments, everyone!" Aunt Louise called. She and a number of the other women had emerged from the kitchen with punch and coffee, platters of sandwiches, cookies and cakes. On the back porch Uncle Paul was probably surreptitiously serving up a stronger drink to the men, Carole thought with a smile.

For a few minutes they all busied themselves filling cups and plates. Carole discovered Dr. Kaufman by her side as she laid a single cookie on the saucer of her coffee cup.

"You're eating so much!" he said to her teasingly.

"Actually, I had a late lunch," she replied.

He gestured toward his own well-filled plate. "I did, too, but I can't resist a spread like this. Home cooking tastes delicious when you eat out all the time."

"Oh?" said Carole inquiringly as, together, they moved toward a sofa set back against the wall of the large living room.

"The fate of an unmarried man," he explained, flashing her another smile.

"I'm enthusiastic about working with you on a volume about the Coldrens," Carole said when they were seated.

"I hadn't expected to enjoy it quite as much as

I'm obviously going to," he replied. "I just wish our association didn't have to be mostly long-distance."

"Oh, that's right. Wimberly College is about fifty miles from here, isn't it?" said Carole. She had looked it up in her atlas before leaving Texas.

"It's more like sixty-five miles when you take into account all the winding mountain roads," he explained. "I do plan to be over here as often as my schedule of classes and conferences permit."

"Good! Because I'm really quite a novice at this, Dr. Kaufman," Carole said with relief. "I've read a lot about folklore, but I've never actually participated in compiling it."

"Oh, it won't be anything very difficult for someone with your writing expertise," he assured her. "If you can get information from people, especially your Aunt Eugenia, on tape, as well as other stories various family members have heard, we can string it all together. By the way, Carole, my name is Tom."

Carole smiled again, pleased by the man's informality. "Tell me, Tom, how did you get started on this project?" she asked.

"In a very old history of North Carolina that I ran across in the Wimberly College library stacks, I read a reference to the bitter enmity between the Coldrens and Haughtons. That book was published in the late 1870s."

She looked up at him, amazed. "Why, that was

before the big shoot-out at the Hilamunga River!"

"Exactly," he confirmed. "At the time I read the old history I was briefly intrigued, but that was nothing compared to my excitement when, in researching another matter entirely, I found a newspaper account about the slaughter by the river. That did it. I started checking various sources and discovered that no one had ever compiled a history of the families or cited any of the reasons for their feud. So I suggested doing that in a grant proposal to one of the historical societies, and, as you know, I received the grant. At first I thought some of my graduate students could do most of the research and legwork, but that didn't work out at all," he said ruefully. "Your Great-Aunt Eugenia clammed up like the sphinx, and Arnold Haughton even got his rifle and threatened to shoot one of my earnest young people!"

"Arnold Haughton? Who is he?" Carole said, startled.

The look Tom Kaufman turned on Carole was equally startled. "Don't you know? Why, Arnold is another eyewitness to the events of April 10, 1899," he explained. "He was a tyke even younger than your Aunt Eugenia, but he saw what happened. I think obtaining his testimony is vital to the book."

"I'm sure it would help," Carole admitted grudgingly, then she stared at the attractive professor in the wake of a dawning suspicion.

"Dr. Kaufman, I was led to believe from Susan's letters that the volume we produced would be about the Coldrens. That it would include the family history with, of course, special emphasis on the long-time feud with the Haughtons."

"Yes, indeed." He nodded. "That's half the project—the part I *know* you can do. It would be wonderful, of course, if you could manage to do the other half as well."

"And the other half?" Carole asked flatly, but already, with a sinking feeling, she knew his answer.

"Why, we've got to include the Haughtons' version, too, in a book of this sort. History, to be accurate, must also be well rounded. Not only would I be greatly criticized if I omitted the Haughtons, but, after all, it's only fair!"

Chapter Three

"It's only fair . . ."

The words of the pleasant professor rang in Carole's mind, but for the next few minutes she was too stunned to make any reply.

He was right, of course. She admitted it. No feud, nor indeed *any* fight, ever had but one side to it. For all the "orneriness and cussedness" of which the Haughtons were capable—at least according to the Coldrens—the Haughtons could no doubt counter with their own incidents and tales of the Coldrens' perfidy.

Why hadn't she realized before, Carole wondered, that for this book to be balanced, parallel stories would have to be written?

Still, it was quite a shock to discover it here and now, when she was too committed to turn back.

I wish I'd known all this sooner, Carole thought, looking away from Dr. Kaufman's clear blue eyes. Yet she also knew she had only herself to blame. Susan's last letter, sketchily outlining the project, had concluded with the sensible suggestion that Carole phone Dr. Kaufman if she had any doubts or questions. But since Carole knew by then that she would be well paid for her work, she'd simply leaped in her car and headed toward North Carolina. *Leaped in with both feet and before looking,* she thought now, a trifle bitterly.

She still wasn't sorry she'd come, but Dr. Tom Kaufman's revelation certainly cast a different light on matters. Also, disappointment was like a keen pang. What writer wanted to be credited with authorship for *half* a book?

Not, of course, that it necessarily had to be that way, according to Tom. "I'll be delighted for you to write the whole volume, Carole, if we can work things out with the Haughtons," he said, sensing her dismay.

"They wouldn't help me in a million years," she answered dolefully.

"Really? You mean hostile feelings still run so high?" He looked at her with a dismay that equaled Carole's. "I've been hoping that with your standing as a professional writer and your having grown up in Texas—"

What he'd hoped for just wouldn't work. Dr. Kaufman didn't know, of course, about that long-ago romance between Carole and Jon Haughton, nor was she about to tell him.

Yet for the Haughtons to let a Coldren—any Coldren—write their family history would take an absolute miracle! Carole knew.

Apparently Dr. Kaufman was a believer in miracles. He advised Carole to use the following day to rest up and make the necessary preparations for her work. Meanwhile he would try again to contact the Haughtons and pave the way toward obtaining their cooperation.

"Let's have dinner tomorrow night," he said to Carole persuasively. "I'll let you know then whether or not I've succeeded."

Carole didn't hold much hope for his success, but she expected to enjoy dining with the professor. And it would be wonderful to have a day off to wash her hair and travel-stained clothes, to check out her cassette recorder and make the necessary arrangements to interview Aunt Eugenia.

"I'll see you tomorrow, then," said Tom Kaufman to Carole and handed over his empty plate to the solicitous Aunt Louise Coldren.

He was the first to leave the party, and his departure proved a signal for the others. They rounded up their children, shook Carole's hand again and bid her farewell. Carole looked at them fondly, thinking that whatever else this writing project involved, she was still glad she'd returned to Green Grove.

She and Susan helped Aunt Louise clear away the clutter of dishes and leftover food, then Carole was alone with the five people who meant the most to her: Uncle Paul and Aunt Louise, Susan and Reggie, and Betsy.

Reggie still held a plate of food, and he urged his thin wife to eat something more. Susan nibbled dutifully at a sandwich, but Carole could tell that she had no appetite and was merely trying to please her husband. From their expressions Carole surmised that they were having trouble over Susan's weight and hoped that it wasn't a truly serious matter between them.

Betsy, by contrast, seemed entirely normal. She was a typical teenager, Carole thought, absorbed in her own thoughts while inwardly alert for the ring of the telephone. Twice it jangled and both times Betsy leaped up before anyone else could make a move.

"Do you have a special boyfriend?" Carole asked her young cousin when Betsy reappeared in the living room, her cheeks flushed and her eyes shining.

"No. I play the field," Betsy replied, her voice carefully casual.

Carole wondered if that was entirely true. One of those phone calls had certainly put a sparkle on Betsy's fresh and pretty face.

A long silence fell, then Carole saw a wave of silent communication pass from Susan to Reggie. Susan cleared her throat. "Carole, I'd better fill you in on the Haughtons, one in particular," she began.

Susan had been Carole's trusted confidante eleven years ago, so, more than anyone else, she knew how serious the romance between Carole and Jon Haughton had once been.

"You don't have to, Susan," Carole said now, striving to keep her voice light. "I've already seen Jon."

Talk about dropping a bombshell! Carole almost laughed at the reaction her words provoked. Everyone went absolutely still from shock. Aunt Louise froze with the coffeepot poised over Carole's empty cup.

Nonchalantly Carole explained what had happened to her car and the accidental encounter with Jon. "So I know he's back in Green Grove and plans to build a dam on the Hilamunga River." Curiously she gazed at the others, wondering why Susan's face was paper-white while color burned along Reggie's cheekbones. "Mr. Haughton bought me lunch, but, after that, things went rapidly downhill. I don't expect to see him again," Carole concluded.

Susan and Reggie's glances slid together. Good heavens, what was wrong with both of them that they kept acting so strangely?

"Carole, I think that's very wise," Susan said after a moment. "Jon Haughton has come strutting back here like some sort of conquering hero! Every single woman in town has been throwing herself at him."

"Face it, dear, for the moment at least he *is* a hero," Uncle Paul said dryly. He turned from his older daughter to Carole. "Jon Haughton is obviously a superb engineer or the state of North Carolina and the U.S. Army Corps of Engineers wouldn't have entrusted him with building a great dam. His presence ensures jobs—a lot of jobs—and that's important in a town like Green Grove, where the economy has been depressed for some time. Of course, I'm as sorry as anyone about Blake's disappointment."

"What disappointment?" Carole said tensely.

"You've seen the shape he's in," Uncle Paul

went on quietly. "Blake's arthritis is the type that's likely to get worse. He can't work as a deputy any longer, so he took an accounting course. Jon Haughton was advertising for accountants as well as secretaries, bookkeepers and so forth. Blake went to apply, but he was never even allowed to put in his application. Jon saw him sitting in the waiting room. He went out and said just two words to Blake: 'Forget it.'"

That certainly didn't sound like the friendly, sweet-natured man that Carole had once fallen in love with. But Jon Haughton's personality had undergone a great change, as she'd already discovered.

"Of course, Jon did hire Lisa Coldren," Reggie piped up. Lisa was a younger cousin who had finished high school a couple of years before, Carole recalled. "After Blake's experience, we told Lisa not to bother, but she's stubborn. She went to see Jon anyway and told him she could type faster than anyone else in Green Grove. So he made her secretary to one of his junior engineers."

"How strange," Carole mused. Why would Jon hire one Coldren after refusing even to interview another? It didn't make sense, but few things about the present-day man did. He was an enigma. She puzzled over it all again later that evening, just before she fell asleep.

Carole awoke the next morning feeling completely refreshed. In the small girlish bedroom, which she'd once shared with Susan, she had slept with her window open to the clean, pure mountain air. It carried with it a tang of pine trees and the sweet aroma of blooming flowers. Now she walked to the window and rested her elbow on the sill, gazing out. Just below her was the huge blue spruce tree that was Uncle Paul's delight. Betsy used to play beneath that tree with her dolls, and once, in the dark there, Jon Haughton had seized Carole in his arms and kissed her so fiercely that her heart had hammered in concert with his.

Watch the memories, Carole, she warned herself, and lifted her eyes to the distant mountains covered with trees and other thick vegetation. Back in those mountains was a primeval forest, as untouched as it was when Indians trod its paths. Great black bear still lumbered about in the wilderness, feasting on berries, hibernating through the winters and emerging in spring hungry, grouchy and trailing two or three new cubs.

Jon had told her all about the black bears, too.

Since every casual thought she had seemed to lead right back to him, Carole reluctantly pulled herself away from the appealing sight of the mountains and got busy with the many chores she had outlined for herself.

Tom Kaufman wore a dark blue suit when he arrived that evening to take Carole to dinner, and the color deepened the blue of his eyes and turned his light blond hair more silvery than before. He was quite a nice-looking man, Carole thought, and she appreciated the way he took her arm to guide her down the walk and into his waiting car.

He, in turn, expressed his appreciation of Carole's attire. Her black silk dress with a ruffle running from neck to waist left her arms completely bare. Its fitted bodice was flattering to her slender figure, Carole knew. Silver high-heeled sandals and a silver shawl completed her outfit.

"There's a new restaurant on the highway that's rather good," Tom said, assisting Carole into his low-slung, raffish sports car. The days of the practical sedan seemed over, Carole reflected, at least with the bachelor crowd.

"That's fine," Carole said, glad that they wouldn't be going to The Cabin, since that was bound to remind her further of Jon.

They spoke little during the drive, just a few remarks about the weather; what a beautiful month May was and how tomorrow should be equally nice when Carole went to interview Aunt Eugenia.

At the elegant and obviously expensive restaurant their conversation turned more serious while they enjoyed glasses of white wine before dinner.

"I've spent the day trying to track down various Haughtons," Tom told Carole, a trace of wryness in his voice. "I understand the hills are full of them, but they're a bit hard to find when they want to be left alone. I did manage to speak at last with Mr. Bryce Haughton and one of his sons, Benjamin. They have a nice place about twenty miles up Rocky Ridge Road."

"Oh, what did they say?" Carole asked, and her hands tightened almost unconsciously on the wineglass she held. Bryce Haughton was Jon's father, Ben his younger brother. She had never seen the homeplace of which Tom spoke so admiringly.

"I think their reaction is best described as lukewarm. They wanted to discuss it with the other family members, particularly one son, Jon. It seems he's the one who's 'made good' and sort of evolved as unofficial spokesman for the family."

This was an even worse development than Carole had expected. She was unable to force one word past her lips.

"So I went to the office of the big man," Tom continued, pausing for a sip of wine. "He's preparing to build a dam, so he's much too busy to see me, according to his secretary."

Carole could only stare at the blond professor and hope that he couldn't detect her inner agitation.

"Just as I was about to leave I heard her confirming a dinner reservation for him. Here. Tonight. At eight-thirty." Tom smiled into Carole's shocked eyes. "I'll bet you didn't know that historians sometimes play spy."

Jon *here*? She would soon be seeing him again! Carole knew she had to say something. Tom sat awaiting her reaction, so she crooked her mouth into a semblance of a smile. "How shrewd of you, Tom. But do you expect him to talk to you at dinner?"

"He may not," Tom admitted, "but I figured anything was worth a try."

Their dinner arrived, but as she looked at her plate, Carole wondered if she could possibly eat. Her appetite had suddenly disappeared.

"Do you know this particular Mr. Haughton?" Tom pressed. "Can you point him out to me when he arrives?"

It was a logical enough question, for the dining room was packed with people. "Yes, I know him," Carole said, her voice low, while her hands dropped to clench the edge of the table. Oh, God, what a mess this was! Jon, who didn't want to ever see her again, was going to be confronted by her in just a few minutes. There couldn't possibly be a worse development! It would positively guarantee his refusal to cooperate.

She would have to tell Tom Kaufman the truth, that she and Jon had once been in love. Perhaps, when he learned about it, he wouldn't want Carole to work on the book at all, because she obviously couldn't be objective, impartial and helpful in winning the Haughtons' cooperation. On the other hand, Tom liked her; Carole knew he did.

Then she saw Jon enter the dining room, and the words she might have spoken dwindled and died away. A tall figure in a beautifully tailored gray pin-striped suit, he dominated the restaurant so completely that Carole heard noises all but cease as people set down their forks and stopped their conversations.

Swiftly Carole's eyes went to the woman at Jon's side. She was pretty and young, with great dark eyes and a soft cloud of black hair that fell over her lilac dress. The sight of them together was like a knife turning in Carole's breast. "Tom," she breathed.

"Yes?" he said, looking up at her attentively.

"Jon Haughton is here," Carole managed, and moved her head in the direction of the handsome man striding across the room.

"Well, well. He does look rather imposing, doesn't he?" Tom said, following Carole's gaze.

"I don't know who the—the lady with him is," Carole forced herself to continue.

"I know her," Tom whispered. "Her name is Lois Wyler and she's a widow with a couple of cute little kids. She works in the courthouse. I met her there while I was going through various old records."

"Oh." The knife in Carole's breast moved just enough to allow her to draw a breath of stabbing pain. Lois Wyler had a sweet heart-shaped face and eyes that were older than her years.

How could you hate a woman like that? Carole wondered. She wanted to jump up, run away and flee from the sight of the two now being seated across the room. If only I can escape before Jon sees me, she thought desperately.

It was too late. His dark eyes skimmed the

room, then stopped on her face. As always she felt his gaze like an almost palpable touch, even as she saw his black eyebrows rushing together.

"Excuse me for a moment, Tom," Carole whispered. She balled up her napkin and dropped it beside her plate.

Tom gave a surprised nod, and Carole fled, cowardlike, to the restroom.

She stayed there for about five minutes until her heart had quit shaking her with its pounding and her knees had steadied. Then, stiffening herself against any more attacks of unseemly emotion, Carole walked back to the dining room with her head held high.

There her eyes swept over the table where she and Tom had been sitting. Instantly she saw that it was empty. Tom was now seated at Jon's table, talking rapidly, judging from the movements of his hands and lips, his face earnest with entreaty.

So he'd gone right over to tackle the big man of Grove County. Carole admired Tom's guts even as a soft sigh escaped her lips.

Tom glanced up and saw Carole. Eagerly he waved her over. She followed on leaden feet, feeling as though she were walking the last mile to her own execution.

Introductions were made swiftly. The young widow flashed Carole a shy smile, and Carole forced herself to smile back. Why would it have been easier if Jon had been with some obvious tramp instead of this pleasant person? Carole wondered dismally.

"So you've turned writer, Carole." Jon's mesmerizing eyes and voice forced her to look up, to see the long column of his neck, his deep-set lustrous eyes and the sensual line of his lips.

"I don't know why I'm surprised," he went on. "You did have a bit of literary ability, I recall, though I would have thought fiction more your forte."

Carole knew immediately to what he referred, and her cheeks stung as though she'd been slapped. Eleven years ago she had written him one ecstatic, loving letter. That letter had been filled with all that a girl's loving heart could convey. Now he had turned it into a bitter joke.

She didn't trust herself to reply, but she could feel Tom's gaze, which held both surprise and curiosity.

Jon turned back to Tom, his voice silky smooth. "While I'm sure your project is commendable, Dr. Kaufman, and that you've undertaken it with the highest motives of historical research and accuracy, I'm bound to think it unwise."

"Why is that, Mr. Haughton?" Tom asked courteously.

"What you—and possibly Miss Coldren, too—have failed to realize is that such a book as the one you envision about the Coldren-Haughton feud will stir up a lot of old feelings: anger, resentment, hatred."

"Oh, surely not, Jon!" The words burst from Carole.

"Oh, yes, surely, Carole," he replied. "Just

what do you think your family and mine have been talking about for the last few weeks? I know what the Haughtons are saying. They're rehashing old fights, sharing memories from parents and grandparents and starting to seethe all over again. I feel like a cook trying to keep the lid on a boiling pot."

"That's ridiculous," Carole cried. "It's uncivilized and downright primitive!" Yet when she remembered the talk around Aunt Louise's table the night before, her heart sank.

"Unfortunately it's human nature to relish gruesome things," Jon went on. His eyes rested on Carole's flushed face for a disturbingly long moment, then his gaze dropped almost burningly to her breasts. She practically ceased to breathe.

He pulled his eyes away and turned back to Tom. "Dr. Kaufman, I've spent the last ten years dodging Indian arrows in Brazil where I built a dam and Arab-Israeli bullets in the so-called Holy Land where I worked on a water recovery project. I've had enough of warfare. I came back to these hills wanting peace and stability for the rest of my life."

"Peace at any price?" Carole inquired acidly. Perhaps it was also peace he'd wanted long ago when he allowed Uncle Buck to scare him away. "You know, Jon, your attitude might be construed as cowardly."

"If so, I can live with the label," he said, his voice very even. "I don't want to get caught in the middle of another war, certainly not one I've inadvertently sanctioned!"

Lois Wyler looked from Carole to Jon with alarm. Then she dropped a small placating hand over Jon's larger one, and at the sight of the gesture, which appeared so loving and possessive, Carole's fury swelled.

"You're not even *curious*?" she said to Jon almost despairingly. "Less than a hundred years ago twenty-one people died in a shootout on the Hilamunga River. To this day no one really knows why, except for a couple of clam-mouthed nonagenarians who might, at last, be persuaded to talk!"

"I have a certain natural curiosity," Jon conceded. "If you ever discover exactly who did shoot Ellen Ann Haughton, I'd be quite interested to know."

Ellen Ann Haughton? Who was she? Carole wondered, and despite her anger with Jon, her own curiosity was aroused.

"Mr. Haughton, are you sure you won't reconsider?" Tom pleaded.

"I won't reconsider." Jon's voice was as implacable as any Carole had ever heard. "The issue is closed as far as the Haughtons are concerned. Now, if you two historians don't mind, Mrs. Wyler and I would like to order our dinner."

"That seems to be that," Carole said glumly. She and Tom had finished their own dinner and left the restaurant. They were now driving back through the quiet town where yellow lights from houses up and down the winding hills spilled out invitingly. Depression gripped Carole. Was it because she'd seen Jon with another woman, an attractive likable woman at that? Or did it stem solely from his refusal to help on the book?

"Oh, I'm not so sure," Tom surprised her by saying brightly.

"*What?*" Jarred out of her lethargy, Carole turned to stare at him. Tom must be the most cheerful man on earth to find anything encouraging in Jon's flat refusal.

In the dim light of the car she could see his smile. "I have two reasons for saying that," Tom told her after a moment. "Mr. Haughton has betrayed interest in a couple of things. One, he wants to know what happened to Ellen Ann Haughton, whoever she may be."

"And the second reason?" Carole probed.

"Second, Jon Haughton is very attracted to you, Carole."

For a moment she was rendered completely speechless by shock. Then, when Carole had regained the use of her voice, she laughed derisively. "You think Jon's attracted to *me*? Oh, Tom, you really are barking up the wrong tree!"

"I don't think so," he said equably. "I'm a man who enjoys the company of women, and obviously, so is he. From the moment he saw you in the restaurant he couldn't tear his eyes away from you. He hardly noticed sweet little Mrs. Wyler, even when she touched him."

"Tom, that's crazy," Carole said flatly. "Jon Haughton dislikes me intensely. He couldn't have made that more evident."

"Sometimes a man appears to dislike a woman because the attraction he feels is unwelcome and close to overpowering," Tom went on sagely.

Carole sat in silence, trying to digest his incredible statements. Were any of them true? she thought doubtfully.

She could feel his sidelong look on her still, stunned face. "By the way," he went on, "I begin to suspect that there might once have been something between you and Jon Haughton. I saw *your* reaction to *him*, too."

For a moment Carole almost hated Tom for his perception and insight. But what did it matter? She had intended to tell him the truth anyway.

"We shared a brief infatuation many years ago," Carole replied, picking her words carefully as she trod through a verbal minefield.

"Ah hah! My dire suspicions are confirmed." His tone poked fun at himself, not Carole. "Want to tell me about it?"

She didn't, but since she saw no escape, Carole briefly recounted her meeting with Jon at the Fourth of July picnic.

"Then, because forbidden fruit is always so desirable, you and Jon soon had a romance astir?" he inquired.

"Something like that," Carole replied. She swallowed against the lump that rose in her throat, longing to cry, *But it wasn't like that at all! We fell in love—madly, wildly, sweetly in love. Yet in light of all that happened later, how could it have been love?*

"What did your aunt and uncle think of your dating Jon?"

"They didn't know at first. Susan was the only one I told. You see, I needed her help. Later, Jean, Connie and the others suspected that I was slipping around to meet Jon Haughton, but you know how closemouthed teenagers are with adults.

"Also," she went on after a moment, "Jon and I really didn't have a lot of opportunities to be together. He was working on a bridge that summer. The construction site was seventy-five miles away over back country roads. At first I saw him only on weekends. Then he started skipping sleep to drive back and forth and see me a couple of nights a week."

"What did the two of you do?" Tom persisted.

Carole wondered what he would say if she told him, "Jon and I couldn't stay out of each other's arms. Usually we parked and made out!" Well, let him guess at that! "Sometimes we went swimming or to a drive-in movie. One Saturday we drove to Asheville to meet an Indian friend of Jon's, Willie Running-Brook." She stopped, suddenly drained by the power of those memories.

"Sounds like it could have been dangerous, a

Coldren and a Haughton growing so close," Tom remarked.

"There was no danger," Carole said, choosing to deliberately misunderstand him. Certainly she'd never been in any *physical* danger. But, oh, the emotional and psychological danger of falling so deeply in love had left scars that marked her still.

"Why did you break up?" Tom asked, stopping his car on the quiet street beside the blue spruce tree. "Did you have a fight or did the kinfolk get wind of it?"

"Nothing so dramatic as that," Carole said wryly. "By the time the adults found out, it was all over, anyway. It just plain fizzled out. Jon went back to building a bridge through the mountains and simply never bothered to call me again." For a moment her hands twisted together in her lap as Carole remembered again the misery of that time. Of going from surprise that Jon didn't call her to consternation, and then to agony.

"I was just a kid," she said after a moment. "I suppose, in retrospect, that he simply lost interest in someone that young and naive."

"Maybe so," Tom said thoughtfully. "Perhaps he's more inclined to appreciate you now. You're certainly the prettiest woman in Grove County."

"How gallant of you," Carole said lightly.

She thought of his earlier remark as they walked to the door. Her chin came up and her jaw clenched with determination. Somehow she was going to find a way to hear Arnold Haughton's memories even if she had to go, alone and uninvited, to wherever the old man lived. For her sake, and Tom's, she was not going to let this project fail!

And there was *something* between her and Jon. She remembered the way his gaze had dropped to her breasts and her own tingly awareness of him.

If Tom were right that Jon found the grown-up Carole desirable, then she had both a weapon and a defense against his overpowering masculinity.

Weapon. Defense. As the words sank into her consciousness Carole gave an involuntary start. Grove County's famous feud between the Coldrens and the Haughtons was obviously still alive between her and the man who had once been her lover. She was beginning to better understand that feud, which made it all the more important for it to be chronicled.

Beneath the porch light, Tom shook her hand and thanked Carole for the pleasant evening. "I'll be eager to know what you learn tomorrow from your Aunt Eugenia," he said, dropping a light hand on her shawl-covered shoulder.

"I'll be happy to tell you," Carole replied readily.

For a moment he lingered, looking down at her almost wistfully, and Carole realized that the professor wanted to kiss her good-night. She saw him decide against it. Instead he gave her hand a final squeeze.

She appreciated his restraint and the obvious importance he attached to their working relationship.

She was finding more things to like about the professor all the time. Yet, for some reason, her mind flew again to Jon.

Chapter Four

 $\mathcal{A}$ unt Eugenia was an early riser, Carole had been told, so at nine the following morning she stopped her car atop a hill outside of town. A neat frame house sat there overlooking the breathtaking beauty of the mountains. The dense blanket of vegetation across the mountains gave off moisture that hung over the slopes in a bluish haze. Later the sun would burn away much of the haze, but now the peaks were still enveloped in mist.

Aunt Eugenia lived with her widowed daughter Edith Sims. Their white house looked newly painted, and the yard had been raked free of any errant leaves. Edith had always been a bit of a fussbudget, Carole recalled, and apparently her advancing age—she was now in her late sixties—hadn't slowed her down.

Cousin Edith had obviously been watching for Carole, for she opened the door before Carole could knock. She was a spry little woman with iron gray hair and flashing brown eyes, still straight and erect, but no bigger around than a rake handle.

"Mama's been up since dawn," she said, leading Carole through the neat-as-a-pin little house. "She's been reading her Bible on the porch, but she's waiting to see you now."

The sun porch was a long low room that afforded an excellent glimpse of the nearby mountains. Aunt Eugenia sat there in a well-cushioned rocking chair, a patchwork quilt over her knees. A large Bible and a magnifying glass lay in her lap.

She was wrinkled and bent and as old-looking as Methuselah, Carole thought as she bent down to drop a respectful peck on one withered cheek. "How wonderful to see you again, Aunt Eugenia!"

"Bet you're surprised I'm still alive and kicking," Aunt Eugenia retorted.

"Now, Mama—," Edith began soothingly.

"I am indeed glad to see you looking so fit," Carole responded. She set down her cassette recorder by the chair Aunt Eugenia indicated she should take.

"You look pretty fit yourself," Aunt Eugenia replied, peering up at Carole with still-keen eyes. "You're a Coldren for sure, for all that you were raised up in Texas by some city-bred mama."

Carole and Cousin Edith exchanged glances, and the older woman rolled her eyes to the ceiling. Carole grinned, glad that their ancient relative's memory was still so alert and intact.

"The day when you were born is written right here in my Bible, Carole Coldren," Aunt

Eugenia went on. "Haven't heard about your getting married, though. You're sure taking your own sweet time about that, aren't you?"

"Yes, ma'am," Carole said respectfully, smothering another grin.

"All the other girls have caught themselves husbands. Wynne's even caught a few too many. Guess I may have to do some husband-hunting for you if you don't get hustling!" Aunt Eugenia threatened. She stopped and pointed a gnarled hand at Carole's cassette recorder. "Well, go ahead and switch that gadget on. I'm ready to tell you what I know."

"Aunt Eugenia, where did the feud begin?" Carole asked, diving abruptly into her subject. "Did it start in Green Grove?"

"Why, it started in Scotland, didn't you know that?" Aunt Eugenia said with some surprise. "As to when, it's so far back I'm not really sure. Sixteenth or seventeenth century—"

"That long ago?" Carole said, startled.

"We're not going to get anywhere, young lady, if you keep interrupting me!" Aunt Eugenia snapped and delivered a light smack on Carole's hand.

"Yes, ma'am," Carole whispered meekly.

"Anyway, that's where we're all from originally. Scotland. It was some wild, outlandish place in the mountains that was cold and wet and dark about half the year. Sutherland . . . that's the name of the north county where we all came from.

"Life there was hard and rough," Aunt Eugenia continued. "I remember my granddaddy talking about Scotland. The Haughtons lived in the nearby hills. If they stole a sheep from us, we'd carry off one of theirs. If they inched over our property line, we'd creep over theirs. There was a lot of dislike between the families even then, stemming from an old Scottish war. Wars do bring out the worst in people."

Aunt Eugenia paused and drew a breath. Then she reached and and patted Carole's hand, the same one she'd earlier smacked.

"I'll tell you all I ever heard about the Coldrens and Haughtons in Scotland on another day," she offered. "But right now it's more important to tell you why twenty-one people died at the Hilamunga River on April 10, 1899."

"Whatever you wish, Auntie," Carole urged.

"At my age, I'm always surprised when I wake up every morning. Since I could pop off any time, I'd better tell you the important stuff first."

"Oh, Mama, don't talk about dying," Edith interjected.

"You be quiet!" the old lady reprimanded her daughter.

Again Edith rolled her eyes to the ceiling, while Carole leaned forward attentively.

Aunt Eugenia gripped the edges of her worn Bible. "Coldrens and Haughtons weren't happy to find themselves neighbors again here in the Appalachians," she said after a moment. "But everybody was used to mountains and loved them, so I guess it was natural they all migrated here, where a lot of earlier Scotch-English immigrants had settled.

"Things went along." Briefly the old lady paused. "The Haughtons stayed in the hills, and the Coldrens moved into town, 'cept it wasn't really a town then, just a little settlement. I guess maybe the old Scottish feud would have been forgotten, except for the Civil War. Count on Coldrens and Haughtons to always choose up opposing sides! The men who came back from that war brought plenty of ugly stories and a lot of hard feelings started up again. I'll tell you more about that, too, on another day, Carole."

Carole twitched in her seat, wondering if Aunt Eugenia was *ever* going to get down to facts. For a few moments the old lady stared off into the distance at some memory that only she could see.

When she spoke again, her voice seemed dry from the accumulation of years. "It was 1898 at the Grove County fair where my uncle, Lucas Coldren, first saw Ellen Ann Haughton. What happened to them, and a lot of others, is what I've remembered all my life!"

The cassette recorder hummed almost inaudibly and the tape spun along on its reel while Carole and Cousin Edith sat transfixed, listening to the reedy old voice of Aunt Eugenia.

"I was just six," she went on, "but I was a smart little girl and just plumb crazy about my

Uncle Luke. He was a tall strapping man of twenty-three or -four, with bright red-gold hair and eyes like black-eyed Susans. Luke always made a big fuss over me, and he did that day, too, at the fair. I was sitting on his knee when one of the Haughton wagons pulled up and he first saw Ellen Ann.

"My, but she was a beauty," Aunt Eugenia breathed. "Slim as a whippet with big black eyes and long raven hair. I've seen prettier women, but never one who seemed more *alive*. A lot of it was the way she moved. Whether she got down off a dusty old wagon or danced around a campfire, that woman was so graceful you could hardly take your eyes off her.

"When Luke saw her, something happened. Just like that. I could feel him staring at her, and after a moment she seemed to feel his gaze, too. She turned and looked square at him, and a sort of surprised look went over her face. Then they both kept on looking at each other like they couldn't turn away.

"Lots of people don't believe in love at first sight," Aunt Eugenia elaborated, "but I saw it happen that day between Luke and Ellen Ann."

"I believe it," Carole murmured, her own thoughts on the day when an almost intangible force had locked her gaze with that of Jon Haughton.

"Luke watched Ellen Ann all that day." For the first time, the old lady appeared to be tiring a bit. "In the evening, when the dancing started, he chose her as his partner. My, but they were a handsome couple, dancing there in the firelight. I guess a lot of other folks noticed it, too, 'cause some whisperings started up right then and there. Those two dancing wanted each other—and it scared the daylights out of both families."

"Oh, good heavens, why couldn't they have left Luke and Ellen Ann alone?" Carole scarcely recognized the cry as her own.

"You don't understand." Aunt Eugenia snapped out of her reverie, and her keen brown eyes swung back to Carole. "Ellen Ann was already married."

"Oh!" Carole gasped.

"She'd been married off at fifteen or sixteen to one of her distant cousins. His name was Haughton, too, but he wasn't good-looking like most of that tribe. Cyrus was twice her age, a rough-looking man with a big bushy beard. He and Ellen Ann had a little boy about four-years-old.

"When Cyrus saw Ellen Ann dancing with Luke, he got furious. He'd been drinking by then—so had most of the other men at the fair—and he stormed over and grabbed Ellen Ann's arm and slapped her face. I saw the way Luke looked. He wanted to kill Cyrus for that, but, of course, he didn't have the right to defend her. She wasn't *his* wife."

Aunt Eugenia fumbled for the handkerchief that lay somewhere beneath her homemade quilt. She blew her nose resoundingly. "I guess both families hoped that ugly scene at the fair had ended it. That Ellen Ann would go back to being Cyrus's unhappy wife, and Luke would never look in her direction again. I know the Coldrens all warned Luke to stay away from that 'witch woman.' That's what they called her. Mountain folks were awfully superstitious, and it was easier to think she'd put a spell on Luke than just to admit that they were two young people who had fallen in love. But it didn't work. Ellen Ann had a lot of resentment toward her husband and a lot of fire in her nature. Luke was high-spirited, too, and he was used to getting what he wanted. They were like two moths drawn into a flame.

"How or where they started meeting, I don't know," the old lady sighed. "In the woods, I guess, or maybe at Luke's cabin. He had his own place—a few acres up on a ridge where he'd built a sturdy cabin. He was ready, you see, for a wife and family."

For a long moment Aunt Eugenia was silent. "And then?" Carole prompted softly.

"I think my grandmama—Luke's mama— knew what was going on, 'cause she was worried sick. I remember one time when she was crying and wringing her hands on her apron and she said to Luke, 'There's going to be trouble if you don't give her up!'

"Anyway, next thing we knew, about six months after the fair, the preacher came down out of the hills one day riding lickety-split and yelling for my daddy and granddaddy. He was a fine old man, and both the Coldrens and the Haughtons respected him. Anyway, he told us that the Haughtons were up in arms 'cause Ellen Ann's brother had just found her body, lying face-down in the Hilamunga River. She'd been shot once, through the heart, and all the Haughtons thought Lucas Coldren had done it."

"My God!" Carole whispered, her heart contracting almost painfully.

"I guess maybe our folks thought at first he'd done it, too. He was young and hotheaded, and, of course, they believed he was bewitched. So they started trying to find Luke. He wasn't at his cabin, but there was blood all over the flooring. No way to tell if it was his blood, or hers, or both of theirs."

"What about her husband?" Carole asked hotly. "I'd think any man who slapped his wife at a fair would be the first likely suspect."

"Other Coldrens thought that, too," Aunt Eugenia said, low-voiced. "But, according to the preacher, it couldn't be him. Cyrus had ridden off to Asheville with a load of furs three days before Ellen Ann's body was found. He'd taken the little boy with him. In fact, the only thing stopping the Haughtons from shooting up the countryside was that they were biding their time till Cyrus got back and learned what had happened to his wife.

"Our men got ready to fight, though they didn't have much spirit for it," she went on.

"They cleaned their rifles and laid in ammunition, but most of all, everybody kept wondering where Luke was. He couldn't have lit out, 'cause his horse was still at his cabin. His wagon, too."

"Where was Luke?" Carole asked.

"It was sickening." Abruptly the old lady stopped to take a breath. "He'd been shot through the head and stuffed down one of the Coldren cousins' wells. They found him after it seemed the well had been poisoned."

Carole flinched and her stomach churned. "So he couldn't have shot Ellen Ann because he was dead himself?"

"Not unless he managed some way to shoot himself in the back of his skull," the old lady replied tartly.

"Then who in the world killed them?" Carole puzzled aloud.

"The Haughtons thought it was the Coldrens, and the Coldrens said it was the Haughtons. Both sides were mad as fire, and there wasn't anything anybody could do, not the women weeping or the preacher quoting the Good Book or all the scared little kids who needed their daddies. . . .

"I know, sure as one can, it wasn't any of our folks who shot them," Aunt Eugenia said thoughtfully. "My granddaddy made every Coldren man lay his hand on the Bible—this Bible I'm holding right here—and swear before God he didn't shoot Luke or Ellen Ann. They all took the oath, too."

"Couldn't one of them have lied?" Carole asked skeptically.

"Not a Coldren! Being honest and God-fearing was a point of pride with us."

"Just as a matter of curiosity, what would have happened if a Coldren man had owned up to the shootings?" Carole inquired.

"The other Coldrens would have killed him on the spot," Aunt Eugenia said flatly. "They would have slung his body over the preacher's horse and told him to take the traitor to the Haughtons and let them see how he'd been dealt with.

"See, there was a code of honor in these mountains that meant something. No matter how the men of both families fought, they didn't kill each other's wives and children. That's why the Haughtons were so all-fired het up over Ellen Ann.

"Of course, after Luke's body was found, the Coldrens were ready to fight, too, and when Cyrus came back with his little boy he started yelling for Coldren blood. The Haughtons began firing across the river. That was the boundary in those days, the Hilamunga River. When they shot Coldren cattle and horses, our men went for their shooting irons. . . .

"Carole, I'll have to tell you about that another day. I'm all tuckered out." Abruptly the old lady stopped speaking.

"Of course, Aunt Eugenia." Carole reached over and touched one of her wrinkled, brown-spotted hands.

"I saw it all," Aunt Eugenia whispered, her voice trembling while tears began trickling down her withered cheeks. "'Course we kids were supposed to stay in the house where it was safe, but a few of us slipped away. We got as close to the river as we dared. We climbed up in the trees and watched what happened." A shudder shook her frail body. "It's a wonder we weren't shot, too!"

When she fell silent and it was obvious that she wasn't going to speak again, Carole leaned over and turned off the cassette recorder.

Shaken by her own daring, Carole parked her car on Green Grove's newest, most exclusive street. It was dusk, the sky a panorama of pink, gold and orange as dark blue shadows gathered and clouds veiled the mountains. Carole still had difficulty believing she was here, outside Jon Haughton's residence. Lying beside her on the seat was a duplicate cassette containing the testimony she'd taken from Aunt Eugenia earlier that day.

She had left the home of the two old ladies shortly after noon, having joined them in a sandwich for lunch. From there she'd gone straight to an electronics store where she had the original tape duplicated, then over to the Green Grove Library, where Susan and Tom had already arranged for her to work in a small office. It was rather bleak and empty-looking, equipped only with a desk, chair and typewriter, but Carole knew it would serve her purpose well.

When she began transcribing the tape the same sense of horror and grief that she'd felt earlier that morning crept over her again. Indeed, it seemed intensified in the library's funereal hush. What a terrible tragedy—what a senseless waste! Because two young people had fallen in love, death had stalked them and their families. Yet surely their story had a moral, too, pointing up the futility of hatred and bloodshed. There was even a continuing mystery, for if the Coldrens hadn't reactivated the feud by killing Ellen Ann and Luke, then who had? The Haughtons?

Now, more than ever, Carole saw the importance of obtaining Arnold Haughton's eyewitness account, and she mulled over this while she typed.

In mid-afternoon the idea sprang full-blown into her mind. If only Jon could hear this tape of Aunt Eugenia's testimony, he might be moved to cooperate.

At first she tried to dismiss the notion. Jon wanted nothing to do with her, he couldn't have made that more evident. I'll look like a fool chasing after him, Carole thought grimly, and she had no desire to worsen his already jaundiced view of her.

But the idea, having seized her, would not let her go. All afternoon Carole's pride warred with her professionalism. A writer on the trail of a story should not be deterred by personal concerns. If there was any way to get this story in its entirety, then she must pursue it! And, after all, hadn't he said that he'd like to know who killed Ellen Ann?

So here she was now, preparing to face Jon once again.

She stepped out of her car and smoothed down the skirt of her neat navy suit. She had changed from the casual slacks and shirt she'd worn earlier, determined to look as professional and businesslike as possible. Beneath the suit a crisp white blouse was buttoned to her throat. At least Jon could scarcely accuse her of trying to look seductive.

It had been easy to learn his address, for it was listed in the latest Grove County telephone book. The sight of his silver Porsche in the driveway, along with an equally new-looking but mud-splattered Bronco, told her that this was obviously the right address.

Before her nerve could desert her completely Carole walked through the sunset's glow to the front door of the new two-story brick house and boldly pressed the doorbell. She heard it chime within.

Nervously she rang the bell again before she received a response. Heels clicked rapidly on a tile floor. The door swung open and she and Jon stared at each other.

His dress was as casual as Carole's was formal. Brown slacks complemented a yellow knit shirt. Its first three buttons were open, revealing a smooth mat of dark curling hair on his chest. On his feet were scuffed, comfortable-looking loafers, only their tassels attesting to the fact that they were an expensive brand.

Jon looked dumbfounded to see her standing there. Then his black eyes gleamed and a derisive smile tugged at the corners of his long mouth. He stepped back and opened the door wide, allowing Carole to enter.

"My goodness, you're full of surprises, Carole," he remarked.

"This isn't what you think, Jon," she said rapidly to hide the confusion that the mere sight of him wrought within her. Already her heart had speeded up alarmingly and her temples throbbed.

"Now, how do you know what I think?" he jibed softly.

How indeed? She decided to let that remark go as she walked inside. To keep from looking at his disturbing presence she glanced around. In the living room a cathedral ceiling vaulted upward, and off to one side stood a curving staircase, leading to the rooms upstairs.

The furnishings were entirely masculine, strong massive pieces made from red oak, maple and other woods native to North Carolina. Indian throw rugs and a few quite striking prints on the wall completed the furnishings. Yet there was an austereness to Jon's dwelling, with everything rather too perfectly in place. On the square coffee table a couple of travel magazines lay positioned with almost military preciseness.

Carole saw the dining alcove out of the corner of her eye, and there, at least, was a bit of disorder. A map lay unrolled on the table, and there was a pad covered with scribbling.

"Am I interrupting anything?" she inquired politely.

"Nothing important." Jon shrugged. "I just knocked off work to have a drink." He stepped close enough that she could detect the faint odor of good bourbon on his breath. "May I fix you one?"

"No. I mean, well . . . all right." Carole realized that she was as tense as a coiled spring. Perhaps a drink would help her to relax.

"Make yourself comfortable," he said, waving her toward the long, low sofa that faced the empty fireplace. "I'll be right back."

Carole sat down on the sofa and drew several deep steadying breaths. For the first time she became aware that soft music played in the background, and she located his stereo set in a walnut cabinet.

Jon returned, his footsteps muffled now by the thick carpet. It was only the entry hall that was tiled, Carole realized. He handed her a tall, cold glass and took a low chair opposite her, sipping on a fresh drink of his own.

"So what have you come about that isn't at all

what I expect?" he began almost teasingly, casually crossing his long, muscled legs.

Carole took a quick gulp of her drink and found it bracingly strong. "I saw my Great-Aunt Eugenia today," she began. "The story she told me concerned the lady you mentioned last night, Ellen Ann Haughton."

"Oh?" His thick black eyebrows drew together thoughtfully.

"I think you should listen to the tape," Carole said. She opened her purse with a click and drew out the duplicate cassette.

"Are you sure you're not divulging family secrets?" he inquired, his lips quirking now in a way that was totally appealing.

"They'll be published in another year or so, anyway," Carole said tightly, wishing that the sight of him didn't affect her heartbeat and respiration so.

"I'm to have a sneak preview? Well, I know you've got something up your sleeve, Carole, but it's a dull evening, so I'm willing to play along." Jon set down his glass, rose and took the tape from Carole.

In a moment the background music was snapped off and the cassette clicked inside the player. Jon returned to his seat, and soon Aunt Eugenia's ancient voice filled the room. As Aunt Eugenia went on talking, his face grew still and, finally, somber.

Although she'd already heard it twice that day, Carole still felt stirred by the story. She took another sip of her drink, her eyes drawn to Jon, and his nearby presence did nothing to still her turmoil.

It was almost unfair that any one man should be so handsome, with such an aura of utter masculinity. Her eyes grazed his thick, crisp hair, just faintly silvering at his attractively hollowed temples. She saw anew the dark, intelligent, almost piercing black eyes. Then there was the long fullness of his beautifully molded mouth, a mouth that she still remembered, with almost painful vividness, covering hers. His healthy male body was beautiful, too, broadchested, slim-waisted, lean-hipped. She remembered being held against that strong chest with her arms locked around his waist, feeling his legs pressing against hers.

Such thoughts were even more disturbing to Carole than the tape spinning out its appalling tale. She forced herself to look away from Jon, staring blindly at an Indian painting on the wall, and kept her gaze rigidly there. She didn't dare look back at him until the tape finally clicked off.

Then, when she did, she was surprised by his reaction. Jon's face had paled, his eyes shadowed by his thick lashes. A light film of perspiration gleamed on his forehead.

"That's quite a story," he said at last, breaking the silence. He picked up his neglected drink and drained most of it in a single swallow.

Carole waited until he looked back at her. Her heart had begun pounding again, and all she'd planned to say to him had gone straight out of her head.

"Why have you come to me with it?" Jon demanded.

"Because now I want to know who killed Ellen Ann as much as you do," she answered, her voice little more than a whisper.

"Why should your interest concern *me*?" he asked bluntly, getting up out of his chair and walking over to stand by the fireplace.

Carole looked up at him, mute with appeal. She could feel her lips trembling. She knew he was testing her, but still his apparent cruelty cut through her like a knife.

"Whatever you think of me, Jon, I think the truth concerns us both. I think it concerns our families, who have spent far too long hating each other and infecting younger generations with that hatred. I think there's a chance now— perhaps the only chance, the *last* chance—to bring forth something good out of bloodshed and tragedy."

He said nothing, only watched her through narrowed eyes.

Shakily Carole got to her feet. He still towered over her, but at least he wasn't quite so intimidating when she confronted him squarely.

"I want your help in obtaining Arnold Haughton's side of the story. I want to learn the Haughtons' version of the feud. I'll let you review all my tapes and notes, Jon, just as I've let you hear this one. I'll let you read drafts of the book as Tom Kaufman and I go along on it. I'll—"

And then Carole could not say another word, for Jon had reached out and seized her.

Chapter Five

*H*is lips crushed down on hers, burning with such a hungry intensity that all Carole's senses reeled. Her heart gave a mighty jolt and seemed to stop from shock, then it began pounding with such ferocity that she felt her ribs being shaken.

His warm, firm mouth plundered hers, first fiercely, then caressingly, but with such daring and fire and abandon that Carole felt herself going limp. Her head swam, her knees threatened to buckle, and just when she thought that surely she would faint from the mad sensations he'd aroused and which were rocketing through her body, Jon gave a muffled exclamation and caught her closer still. Giddily Carole realized that her feet were being swept off the floor and she was supported entirely by his arms, which felt as though they were trembling, for all their fierce strength.

His mouth on hers turned softer. He was kissing her now in the same tender yet passionate way she had remembered through several thousand lonely empty nights.

Carole's hands moved upward to link around

his neck, and she could not have moved if the world had exploded then and there. With his kisses gone so tender, she was utterly helpless to resist him. She had dreamed of this too long and had wanted it—wanted *him*—too badly. Now she could only respond with a fiery abandon of her own.

Carole's hands twined in Jon's hair, and she found that she was gripping him almost as tightly as he held her. His crisp hair clung magnetically to her fingers, curling over them.

His lips moved to rain kisses across the smoothness of her cheeks, ranged upward to her temples, then downward to her throat, where she could feel the heat of his ragged breathing. Her own was just as uneven. "Oh, Jon!" Carole heard herself gasp. "Jon!"

Slowly, tantalizingly, his mouth glided lower, pressing soft kisses against her neck. She felt his tongue dart across that slim column of flesh, tasting her skin and savoring it, as though he found her delicious.

Jon's hands began to move in concert with his lips, stroking and pressing a random pattern across Carole's back. His fingers traced her shoulder blades, then delicately explored her backbone. Wherever he touched, whether with lips, tongue or hands, her body gave a joyous quiver of response. Beneath Carole's staid, prim clothes each atom of her body, now awakened by Jon, sang with vibrant life.

His moist open mouth nibbled back up her neck to her earlobes. With teasing nips he tasted and feasted there. Carole had forgotten how sensitive earlobes could be until she felt Jon's thorough search. His tongue flashed inside one petal-shaped ear, and she moaned with delight.

His head moved to Carole's other ear, arousing and awakening it in the same way, while his massaging fingers dipped lower on her back. Briefly they encircled her waist, then she felt them outlining the soft swell of her hips. Jon's hands continued on to find the small sensitive hollow at the base of Carole's spine. Abruptly he pulled her closer still, until she fit magically against his muscular thighs. Now his hands cupped the roundness of her smooth buttocks and lingered there, the arousing fingertips sliding like fiery tendrils across her welcoming flesh.

Raw excitement burst like a rocket inside Carole. "Oh!" she sighed. Had his arms not supported her she would have sagged to the carpet in ready compliance with his every wish.

"Shh," Jon whispered, his lips poised only inches from hers. His face was so close she could see the fine pores of his skin, could count each separate black hair of his eyebrows. Then his mouth closed over hers again with such insistent thoroughness that Carole's last rational thought fell away. His mobile lips fitted on hers so perfectly that she grew even more intoxicated with desire. Again and again Jon kissed her with unbelievable softness and yearning.

Jon was the one who broke the embrace at last, wrenching away from Carole as though it took every ounce of his strength to do so. He leaned back against the fireplace, as if needing its marble support, while Carole tried dizzily to maintain her balance on a floor that appeared to be rocking.

"So you need my help?" His voice emerged so sternly that had it not been for her still-burning lips and body, reminders of him, Carole might have quailed before his tone.

She managed to nod and felt the jerkiness of her movement. Her arms, she realized in some surprise, were still outstretched to him. Carefully she lowered them to her sides.

"Then let's talk of practical matters, Carole."

His voice had steadied, she realized through her own swimming senses. It was not so abrasive, yet his eyes glittered almost alarmingly.

"Practical matters?" she managed to repeat.

"Yes. I am, after all, a very busy man, with a dam to build. The other night Dr. Kaufman explained that you were being well paid to undertake the research and writing of this book. Now you've asked that I give up quite a bit of my valuable time to assist you. Just what, may I ask, are you proposing to offer for my assistance?"

Carole stared at him numbly. Then her blanked-out mind began to function again, and she felt a deep crushing sense of disappointment. "I don't know what you want, Jon. If it's money, you'll have to discuss that with Tom Kaufman."

"Oh, it's not money," he said emphatically,

"and what I want only you can deliver. I still want *you*, Carole. God knows why, but I do—and you want me, too. That much is obvious. So why not spend a few nights in my bed? That will ensure my cooperation."

Now Carole feared she really would faint. Fortunately, anger began to tingle through her veins, bringing her to a cold, conscious awareness of her surroundings. "What do you think I am, Jon?" she cried hotly.

"I think you're a woman who was about to do for pleasure what you now so indignantly refuse to do as payment. Really, Carole, that seems quite inconsistent."

She saw the cynical expression on the face she'd thought so handsome only moments before, and now a sense of sickness came to join with the anger filling Carole's breast.

"You're crazy," she whispered hoarsely. She darted to the sofa, she snatched up her purse and then started for the door. Something stopped her there, causing her to turn around and look at him once more.

Jon was still in the same position, leaning against the mantel. His face looked taut from some emotion she could not even begin to fathom.

"I don't know what's happened to you, Jon," Carole gasped and now tears of hurt weren't far away. The quiver of her voice warned her. "You used to be so kind and gentle—"

"And you were a damned fine little actress even then, Carole. But when the chips were down, you ran squalling to the Coldrens! You know you did!"

"I—I *never*—" she gasped.

"Your Uncle Buck was well informed. He even knew we'd made love. Since I didn't tell him, should I bother to ask who did?" Jon said scornfully.

Carole knew who had, and even at this late date she almost died from shame and embarrassment. It could only have been Susan—skinny Susan—but there was no arguing that with the angry, bitter man before her. Jon's face revealed quite plainly that he was not prepared to believe anything she said.

She fumbled for the door knob and managed to turn it. Then Carole plunged out into a night no longer soft with twilight but black and foreboding.

From the man she left behind her came a sound just as dark and foreboding, the sound of his harsh laughter.

If Carole had ever spent a more pain-filled night, she didn't remember it, and she'd known quite a lot of bad nights. But even in the worst of her anguish she had usually been able to cry herself to sleep. Now she was dry-eyed, her mind still in an uproar as she tried to puzzle out just who and what Jon Haughton had become. Surely his bitterness didn't stem solely from a brief conversation with Uncle Buck Coldren years ago, especially since he could have defied Uncle Buck so easily. No, Carole knew she must look deeper than that, however much she herself might regret her misplaced confidence in Cousin Susan.

Had Jon worked so hard to become a successful, sought-after engineer that he'd grown completely mercenary and grasping? Or had the tragic death of the girl he loved caused a wintry chill to be born in him, ultimately freezing off all human feelings?

Whatever it was, something had happened to change the man she'd once known, an eager young man, vital with life, who loved mountains and clear streams . . . and Carole Coldren.

Apparently that man was gone, outgrown or discarded, as dead as Ellen Ann Haughton, who'd been shot through the heart. Some part of Carole could still not relinquish his memory without grief.

When he'd kissed her tonight, when his mouth had turned so softly passionate, she'd felt as though her old lover had returned. But that was all deception, a lie as cruel as his eyes and voice.

Restlessly Carole tossed in the narrow twin bed, pounded her pillow, and tried to sleep, but rest eluded her.

Part of it, she knew candidly, was her body's lack of fulfillment. Her body didn't *care* what Jon had once been and now become. It wanted only to be joined again with his.

Subduing the hungry human flesh had tested even saints, Carole remembered, and she certainly wasn't any saint, just a normal healthy woman who had lived too long without a man. Without Jon.

At last, just before dawn, she finally dropped into exhausted slumber, but later she was sorry she had slept at all, because her unconscious mind, fueled by her body's frustrated yearnings, set her dreaming, and she relived the way it had been between her and Jon on a single, star-spangled night late in July. . . .

That night she had slipped down the stairs after the house was still, tiptoeing past the den where Uncle Paul still watched TV. Carole had eased the back door open and then dashed across the lawn where Reggie Briggs's old Plymouth sat parked and empty, the keys tucked under the front seat.

Susan had earlier made the arrangements for Carole to use Reggie's car. Guiltily, Carole put the Plymouth into neutral and coasted down the quiet street. Rounding the corner, she finally dared to start the engine and switch on the lights. Then she drove, as fast as she could, in the direction of Morgan's Cove.

Carole had hated slipping around like that almost as badly as Jon had. He had threatened to march boldly up to her front door and introduce himself to Uncle Paul and Aunt Louise, calling for Carole openly. Yet Susan had been adamant that such forthrightness would be the worst possible tactic.

"If the family finds out you're seeing Jon

Haughton, they'll pack you right home to Texas!" she'd warned Carole. And Carole, frightened more by that possibility than any other, had managed to prevail on Jon to do what Susan suggested.

It wasn't a long drive to Morgan's Cove, and as she turned onto the road that wound around the wide, grassy pasture set between mountains Carole marveled anew that the word "cove" had such a different definition here. The only water at Morgan's Cove was a clear, narrow stream. To the mountain people a cove was a small valley, and this was a particularly lovely one by day.

Then Carole saw the familiar truck Jon drove parked just off the road, and his headlights flashed, a welcome beacon. She forgot about everything but the man who awaited her. Quickly she stopped.

Jon's truck door swung open, and he alighted when Carole did, running toward her, his arms opening to enfold her. Carole rushed straight into those welcoming arms, and when his lips came down on hers she could believe that people sometimes died from sheer glorious happiness.

Over the past several weeks their kisses had grown steadily bolder, their hands on each other's bodies more searching and eager. But that night, as they lay together on a bed of mosses and ferns, Carole felt herself being transported into a new adult world of delight.

Carefully Jon had lifted the weight of Carole's

silken hair away from her neck to rake his tongue along the tender skin usually hidden there. She shivered ecstatically, aware of his growing excitement and as stirred by it as she was by her own.

His breath came in rasps as his lips roved tenderly back to press against her collarbone, while his hands eased open the first button of her V-neck blouse. Then his mouth and tongue moved over the delicate skin of her upper chest while his hands gradually eased her blouse from beneath the waistband of her jeans.

"I love you so, Carole Coldren!" Jon breathed, and Carole's senses stirred, both from the passionate intensity of his words and the sudden touch of his skillful hands across the bare skin of her waist. His touch was feather light, his fingers splayed as they began a gradual seductive ascent toward her breasts. Ten tiny firecrackers of arousing warmth, followed by the smooth glide of his palms, electrified her.

Jon's lips moved steadily downward even as his hands continued their progressive rise. For the first time in her life Carole became sensually aware of her breasts and their potential for excitement. They grew strangely heavy, tingling at the anticipated assault by Jon. Unconsciously Carole's lips parted, and her head fell back, thrusting her chest eagerly forward.

Jon's black head was buried now in the opening of her white blouse and the contrast in the moonlight between dark and light filled Carole with a new, strange and almost unbearable longing.

His desirous lips, warm and wet, reached the slopes of her breasts as his hands began tenderly kneading their undersides. The impact on Carole's emotions increased to alarming proportions. She gave a soft moan deep in her throat while her breasts moved and stirred beneath his touch.

"Do you like that?" Jon whispered huskily, his hands at last cupping those warm mounds.

"Oh, yes!" Carole whimpered, aroused almost beyond speech by the delicious circular movements of his palms.

"May I kiss them?" Jon said, and without waiting for her assent, his mouth dropped over one tingling globe.

Carole's soft, ecstatic cry was his signal to proceed. Rapidly, yet without any appearance of great haste, he loosed the last few buttons, opening her blouse wide and slipping it down off her arched shoulders. Quickly his hands slid around Carole's back, finding the clasp of her bra. A moment later the bra fluttered down beside her blouse, discarded on the grass.

Jon's lips closed softly over one taut nipple, and Carole's breath began coming in shallow pants. He directed his attention to its twin, his hands never still, but stroking and caressing even as his mouth continued its gentle plundering. He kissed her nipples, laving them with his tongue, until Carole felt herself going a little crazy. "Don't stop!" she managed to whisper, holding his dark head to her glistening breasts.

Slowly Jon drew one crescent peak full into his mouth, tugging at it, then suckling firmly. The motions created a small explosion within Carole, unleashing a flow of lava. For the first time she felt a primitive ache beginning deep inside her body.

While Jon's mouth moved between her breasts his hands dipped lower to stroke her waist and stomach. In the warm night, silent except for their heavy breathing, Carole clearly heard the zipper of her jeans being opened. Then his hands were fondling her stomach while impassioned words tore from him.

"Carole, you'll have to stop me—I can't stop myself!" Jon groaned, his face buried in the softness of her bare breasts. "I want you too much!"

"I want you, too, Jon!" It was all Carole could say as her fingers raked his hair, then ran eagerly down the length of his spine. She felt his pleasurable shudder beneath her gentle touch, then he was pulling her jeans away from her legs and caressing her belly and thighs until she writhed with desire.

Jon knelt by her ankles and began running his hands over them, then up the length of her legs. When his lips followed in damp, warm kisses Carole felt the throbbing deep inside her moving beyond an ache to a fierce clamor. His thrilling fingertips glided up the insides of her legs until they reached the juncture of her thighs. Jon kissed the soft skin there deeply with scorching breath.

Carole felt herself quivering all over, and her reaction appeared to further enflame Jon. Suddenly his hands were beneath the waistband of her thin panties, then they, too, disappeared into the night.

"How lovely you are! And how much I love you!" Jon said fiercely, catching the length of her naked body against him. Beneath his own clothes Carole felt a masculine hardness when he pressed against her. Rather than being frightened by his evident need, Carole gloried in his response.

In just a few more seconds Jon drew away to discard his own clothes. Fleetingly Carole saw him outlined in the moonlight, and although she had never before seen a man nude—had, indeed, learned of the male anatomy only through statues shown in art books—she thought Jon's body was glorious.

When he returned to her arms she marveled at the perfect fit of their bodies and the contrasts between masculine and feminine. His chest, lightly matted with soft hair, pressed against her yielding breasts. His strong, straight, muscled legs meshed with her softly curved ones. Things that had puzzled Carole about her own body suddenly came clear when she saw their complementary opposite in Jon.

She drank from his lips until he sighed in satisfaction, and they drew closer and closer still. Finally, Carole felt his bare knee edging her legs apart. "I don't want to hurt you," he whispered against her avid lips.

She knew he wouldn't and he didn't. Jon was very gentle entering her, slowly easing deeper into the secret passage that welcomed him. Then, as their bodies fused, passion caught them urgently in an almost violent grip. In love and trust they moved together in a rhythm as old as time, building and straining to the final ecstatic culmination.

Later, Jon was the more remorseful. "I shouldn't have, Carole! I knew you were a virgin." Stricken, he turned to reach for his clothes.

She caught him close, soothing him wordlessly as she smiled into the night. How could something so natural and rapturous possibly be wrong?

"You're so young in so many ways," Jon went on agonizedly, "even if you are nineteen."

That was the only lie she'd ever told him, increasing her age by two scant years, since she had feared he might otherwise have lost interest in her.

"I'm not sorry, Jon," she whispered against his crisp, clean-smelling hair. "I love you and I—I thought it was beautiful!"

"Oh, sweetheart, do you really *mean* that?" he said, turning back to her. Then, reading her face in the moonlight, Jon leaned down to Carole again, and soon he forgot all about getting dressed.

It was less than two hours before daybreak when Carole finally returned home. Jon had followed, to be sure she arrived safely, and to claim one last passionate kiss under the great blue spruce tree. Then Carole threw a handful of gravel at Susan's window to awaken her cousin. Immediately a light flashed on in the bedroom, and Carole knew Susan was on her way down to the kitchen to unlock the back door that Uncle Paul would have bolted so carefully after he finished watching TV.

Only when she stepped into the cozy kitchen did Carole realize how she must have looked after the long night of lovemaking. "I've been worried sick, Carole!" Susan began chiding. Then she stopped, peering at Carole's radiant face while color drained from her own.

"Oh, no!" Susan whispered in stark terror, and Carole knew that any denials would be futile. Susan could plainly see what had transpired that night between a Coldren and a Haughton.

Oh, yes, she still remembered just how it had been eleven years ago. Carole remembered too much and too well. But now the man she'd once loved had become a stranger. Or had that coldly calculating streak been a part of his nature all along? Perhaps he'd secretly enjoyed deceiving and seducing a Coldren woman.

When she looked at her tired image in the mirror the next morning, Carole saw a new hardness in the set of her eyes and mouth.

Though her body and her subconscious mind might combine to betray her with dreams, she vowed that she was through with Jon Haughton forever. He'd insulted, rejected and disdained her in every way that a man could.

For a moment Carole seriously considered abandoning this whole project. It certainly appeared doomed to failure without the Haughtons' cooperation. Why, she could pack her car and be back in Houston——

No! Her professional pride stung, she set her mind against it. She had never abandoned an assignment before; she wasn't going to start now. She would fulfill her side of the agreement, at least.

Dressed casually in slacks and a tunic shirt, Carole went down to breakfast. Uncle Paul had already gone to his office downtown, but Aunt Louise was still bustling around the kitchen. Betsy sat at the table, munching dreamily on a muffin.

"Heavens, Betsy, hurry up!" Aunt Louise urged the girl. "You're going to be late for school."

"Oh!" Betsy gave a start and dropped the muffin in her plate. She sprang up, looking as fresh as the May morning, her long hair brushed and gleaming, her face aglow. She dashed out with a barely mumbled "Good morning" to Carole.

"That girl," Aunt Louise grumbled, turning back to the stove. "I don't know what's gotten into her lately. If I didn't know better, I'd say she was in love."

"Maybe she is," Carole suggested, taking the seat that Betsy had just vacated.

Aunt Louise shook her gray head. "She doesn't date anyone in particular. Of course, there may be someone she likes who hasn't noticed her yet. Oh, Carole—" In a rapid change of subject, Aunt Louise informed her that Tom Kaufman had phoned the previous evening. "I think he wanted to know what you've learned from Aunt Eugenia."

"I'll call him today," Carole promised as Aunt Louise set a plate before her. Although she had little appetite, Carole made herself eat the nourishing breakfast of juice, toast and scrambled eggs.

Later she went to her small office at the library. It had been agreed that to avoid overtaxing aged Aunt Eugenia, Carole would interview her on alternate days. So she busied herself with starting a narrative and making notes of questions she wanted to ask Aunt Eugenia the next day. Though her head throbbed with weariness from her nearly sleepless night, Carole worked steadily until noon, when she was joined by Tom Kaufman.

Tom listened to the tape, then took Carole to lunch. While they sat over chef's salads Carole gave him an abbreviated report on her work and her futile attempt to interest Jon Haughton in it.

"Just do the best you can," Tom urged her.

Carole went back to the library and worked steadily until three. By then sheer weariness threatened to overtake her. She decided to go back home and take a short nap before dinner.

When she walked out of the library and started toward her car, Carol was amazed to see the silver Porsche also parked there. Its door opened and Jon Haughton stepped out.

Carole went rigid, and despite all her resolutions, her heart speeded up at the sight of him. The afternoon sunshine burnished his ebony hair with auburn highlights, and he looked devastatingly handsome in a black business suit, snowy dress shirt and crimson tie.

Carole stared at him wordlessly while Jon walked toward her. Despite her inner turmoil, she was determined to shield herself against any further attacks. She felt her chin jerk up and knew her eyes must be glacial. Curious, she awaited whatever he might say.

Jon stopped before her and his hands moved in a deprecating gesture of . . . what? Carole wondered. Was it supplication? Apology?

"I'm sorry, Carole," he said quietly. "I know I was a boor last night. I'd been drinking, as you know—"

He hadn't appeared to be drunk or even slightly loop-legged, her cool brain pointed out. Nor was Carole in any mood to accept his apology.

"You suggested I sell myself to assure your cooperation," she said, her voice tight. "I resent what that implies."

"I don't blame you." Jon's voice turned smoother. "I rarely drink to excess. I hope you'll pardon me for it."

"Frankly, I don't feel inclined to," Carole said, stung to anger, although something in her midregion insisted on aching. "I don't know what I've ever done to give you such a low opinion of me. Of course, I shouldn't have talked to Susan about us, but teenage girls have talked to best friends since the beginning of time—"

"Let's don't talk about the past," he interjected swiftly. "That's over and done with, even if I, too, tend to forget at times. The real issue is today. You're writing a book, Carole, and you asked for my help. I've decided to provide it—if you still want it, that is."

"I don't know, Jon." Carole looked up at him and tried to remain unaffected by the sight. "After last night, I don't see how it would be possible. Besides," she went on remorselessly, "what's your reward?"

A smile lifted the corners of his long mouth, his acknowledgment that Carole's shot had been good. "You can forget my earlier outlandish suggestion," he assured her. "All I ask is the opportunity to do exactly what you offered last night, with one exception."

"What's the exception?" Carole demanded suspiciously.

He hesitated again, briefly. "I have to protect my family's interests. Tapes and notes can always be doctored."

"If you think that I—" Carole started heatedly.

"No, you misunderstand!" Again Jon cut in hastily. "I don't think that, but certain other family members might. So I'll have to ask to accompany you on all interviews, just that, as well as have the opportunity you've already offered to review your tapes and notes."

"And your pay for all your valuable time?" She couldn't resist pursuing this sorest of all subjects.

"I've decided to consider it a contribution to academia, if you will. To historical research and accuracy, et cetera."

Carole drew a deep breath. Don't believe him, her mind advised. He could probably sell snake oil to a physician! "It wouldn't work," she said tiredly.

She felt his eyes running over her face and knew that weariness and depression were etched there. Reluctantly she looked back up at him and noticed what she'd missed earlier, that he looked almost equally tired.

"Give me a chance, Carole," Jon said, low-voiced. "If I can't undo my disastrous actions of last night, at least I can prove that that isn't the only side of me. I *can* help you. You know it or you wouldn't have come to see me last night. Uncle Arnold will be a tough nut to crack under the best of circumstances. He's a strange duck, almost a recluse. Fortunately, he's rather fond of me."

"I don't know why you want to help me," Carole said, but already she knew she was wavering. Jon's assistance would be absolutely invaluable, she knew.

"Why, I've already told you." He smiled. "I have a burning curiosity to know who killed Ellen Ann Haughton—and now Luke Coldren as well."

Almost against her will, Carole felt her eyes lured upward again to his. Jon's looked much softer today, no longer glittering like hard, cold, black marble. Oh, if only he would always look at me like this! she thought wonderingly.

He saw her indecision and reached over to take her arm. His touch was gentle, almost respectful, yet warmly thrilling.

"Let's go have a cup of coffee and talk about it," he suggested.

Carole wasn't quite sure how it had all come about, but somehow the arrangements for her working with Jon had been smoothly and easily worked out. Though she wondered warily if she would regret allowing Jon to participate, there was still a stubborn spark inside her that would not die, a spark that had always responded to Jon.

He was at her door bright and early the next morning, for Carole had told him to call for her there. She was no longer a tremulous girl of seventeen, fearing exile to Texas. At twenty-eight, she could drive off with whomever she pleased. Still, Jon's appearance had thrown Aunt Louise Coldren into quite a flurry. There might be an even worse flurry when she returned, Carole realized, but she could handle it now.

Young Betsy had been quite intrigued. "Oh, golly, he's so handsome!" she breathed while Carole scooped up her notebook and cassette recorder. "He looks like—oh, one of the guys I know at school."

Eager as she was to be off and away with Jon and escape Aunt Louise's reproachful stare, Carole glanced at her sixteen-year-old cousin. She knew the young man to whom Susan referred, and she wondered just how friendly the girl really was with Terry Rodgers.

Then she forgot all about her family members in her sheer exuberance. It was a beautiful morning, still cool, but bright with sunshine. The mountains were not so hazy this time. Green and majestic, they soared toward the sky.

Jon was on his best behavior, Carole noted with relief. He was polite and attentive, asking if she were comfortable and whether she found the car too warm or cool. He was dressed casually in charcoal slacks, a lighter gray shirt open at the throat and a soft blue V-neck sweater.

Carole's beige linenlike suit was more summery. Beneath her jacket she wore a turquoise silk shirt. Unconsciously her hands moved between the twin strands of gold at her neck.

"Such mighty forests," she murmured, tearing her eyes away from the sight of him sitting so easily beside her. She looked out at the great stands of timber instead.

"Yes. More than forty percent of the forests are virgin wood," Jon answered. "The creation of all the parks and wildlife refuges saved the state from further plunder by the axe and saw."

"I'm glad," she said. "I wish I could stay here forever!"

"Maybe you can." Though emotions played across his face, his voice was carefully noncommittal.

"Oh, I'm sure I'll have to go home when this project is finished. Unless, of course, it leads to my doing others that are similar," she replied.

"Would you like that?" Jon asked.

"Yes. It's the most rewarding work I've ever done," Carole confided. Then she saw that they were nearing a highway intersection. "Turn right up ahead, Jon. Go two miles down the blacktop. Aunt Eugenia and Cousin Edith live at the end of that road."

He executed the turn and followed her instructions. "I'm a bit curious as to how your older relatives will receive me," he said when they pulled up before the neat white house of Edith Sims.

"And how will yours receive me?" Carole questioned.

Jon answered with an eloquent shrug of his wide shoulders. "Guess there's only one way we'll find out, isn't there?"

When Carole introduced Jon, Edith Sims's brown eyes shot sparks. "I don't know what Mama's going to say about this," she warned.

Carole turned anxiously toward Jon, but he wore his most dazzling smile. "If she objects to my presence, Mrs. Sims, then certainly I'll leave. But I hope she won't mind. I've heard so much about her from Carole." His glance swept the tidy living room. "What a pleasant place you have."

Before her eyes, Carole could see Cousin Edith beginning to thaw. She led them out to the sun porch where Aunt Eugenia waited.

"Land sakes, I thought I was dreaming," she said on sighting Jon. "It's been so long since I've heard a man's voice in this house. My, you're a fine-looking one, too!" Aunt Eugenia turned to regard her great-niece. "Where did you find this bonny lad, Carole?"

Carole knew she was coloring under Aunt Eugenia's gaze and Jon's amusement as well. "Why, right here in Green Grove, Auntie," she answered lightly.

"His name is Jon Haughton, Mama," Cousin Edith interjected.

"It is, huh?" The lively old eyes took on added interest. "Step closer, young fellow, and let me have a better look at you."

Jon smilingly complied and Aunt Eugenia gave a snort of satisfaction. "Yes, you're a Haughton all right. Dark as crows, all of you. That's what my daddy used to say."

"And *my* granddaddy used to say the Coldrens all had hair like fire and skin like a frog's underbelly." Jon laughed.

Aunt Eugenia stared at him for a moment, then began to cackle. "That's a good one. I think I'm going to like you, boy. Sit down."

Carole bit her lip against her own nervous laughter. At least the tense atmosphere had relaxed, but she wondered when Jon had last heard himself referred to as a "boy."

Actually he did look younger today, with his shirt open to reveal the long line of his throat. His hair was tousled slightly, and his eyes brimmed with interest and mirth. Carole forced herself to look away from the appealing sight he made, sitting on the hassock at Aunt Eugenia's feet. She set up her cassette recorder and switched it on.

Today Aunt Eugenia's stories ranged back to Scotland and what she'd heard as a small child from her parents and grandparents. Sometimes she was blunt, as she talked about raids and skirmishes in the Highlands that had further inflamed the two families' dislike of each other, but she also exhibited a surprising amount of tolerance.

"Now, I'd be glad to know what your folks have said about that, Jon Haughton," she remarked on finishing one tale. "Guess they'd tell a different version."

"Probably," Jon conceded dryly. "Carole and I will have to check that out."

"Frankly, the Coldrens' story always sounded a mite fishy to me," Aunt Eugenia admitted, and Jon laughed once again, his voice relaxed and youthful.

When she'd finished relating the Scottish tales and Carole had clicked off the recorder, Aunt Eugenia turned with frank liking to Jon. "Come back another day with Carole," she offered.

"I'd enjoy that," Jon said, rising easily and leaning over to take one of her liver-spotted hands.

An intangible communication seemed to pass between the two people, separated by sixty years of age and generations of family hatred. Suddenly Jon bent down and dropped a light kiss on Aunt Eugenia's wrinkled cheek. "I appreciate your courtesy, ma'am," he said sincerely.

Watching him, Carole felt a strange pang in her breast. When Jon was like this, how difficult it was to resist him!

Of course, he's a born charmer, she thought a few minutes later when she saw him defrost Cousin Edith completely. The two elderly ladies, lonely for companionship and missing contact with menfolk, would welcome him back.

She and Jon walked slowly toward his car. "Thank you for being so nice to them," Carole said softly.

Jon turned a look of astonishment on her. "It's not really my practice to badger old ladies," he said, his voice amused.

Before she could reply he reached down and

took her hand. "Or young ones, either," he added ruefully, his thumb tracing a lazy circle in her palm.

Carole felt her pulse leap when Jon's fingers linked through hers. Just the mere touch of his skin on hers was exhilarating. Slowly he raised her hand to his lips. "Thank *you*, Carole," he said, low-voiced, "for the opportunity to be here. You were right—I should be."

His warm lips brushed the top of her hand, then he turned it over gently and pressed a far more lingering kiss on the inside of Carole's wrist. Her pulse gave such an ecstatic bound that she wondered if Jon had felt it, too.

There was no way for Carole to know, but, instinctively, their other hands entwined, too. For an endless moment their gazes locked and held as Jon looked down deeply into Carole's eyes. Her own uplifted gaze was riveted to his.

The same sheer boyish joy that, once, had always brimmed in Jon's dark eyes now shone through again. Their linked hands were those of equals and, possibly, even friends.

How many times can I lose heart, Carole thought wonderingly, only to take heart again! She didn't know, but she found herself swaying toward Jon invitingly.

After a moment's brief hesitation he accepted the invitation. His arms went around her lightly, and Carole felt her own seizing him. Carefully, Jon drew her closer. He held her loosely, resting his chin against the top of her hair. Carole felt that touch as though it were a laser.

It radiated through her hair and skin to lodge deep within.

Such undemanding tenderness on his part was just what she needed at the moment. Carole's own arms locked behind Jon's back while the bruises he'd inflicted on her very soul began to mend. He had urged her to give him another chance. Now she was glad that she had.

Beneath her cheek she could feel Jon's strong heartbeat. Indeed, Carole felt it accelerate gratifyingly with their embrace, but he made no further move. He didn't attempt to kiss her or caress her. He just held her, held her so comfortingly close and near. It was a quiet time of truce and peace-keeping. Though Carole had no illusions that it could last—oh, how good it felt for the moment!

Somewhere in the house behind them a window shade flew up. Suddenly aware of what they were doing, locked in this silent yet intent embrace, Carole drew away embarrassed, her face flushing.

Jon didn't appear to notice Carole's chagrin as he guided her over to the passenger side of his car.

Chapter Six

$\mathcal{N}$ow where?" Carole asked too brightly, settling into the seat beside Jon, a seat that was becoming quite familiar to her.

It was the following morning, for Jon had explained that he could spare only half a day at a time for their outings. The only reason he had any free time at all at present was because the younger engineers had not yet supplied information he needed for the dam. Carole knew she should be grateful that her arrival had coincided with a lull in his usually busy schedule.

But today she was conscious only of her own inner tension and confusion. What on earth had thrust her into his arms yesterday? Yet she knew that at his first small gesture of tenderness she had invited the subsequent embrace.

Carole was not used to being baffled by her own behavior. Nor did she know why Jon Haughton, of all the men she had known, could turn her into such a weak, willing and witless woman! Her overly bright greeting had sounded phony even to her own ears.

Mercifully, Jon showed no awareness of

Carole's discomfort. Rather, he readily answered her question of where they would go.

"Today it's my turn," he said thoughtfully. "I tried to phone Arnold Haughton last night—'Pop Arnold' is what we call him—but he didn't answer. Of course, he might have been working outside. He's still quite active and spry.

"On the other hand, he probably just ignored the phone," Jon went on. "He never wanted one in the first place, but the family insisted, because of his age. A lot of times when he does answer, he'll say, 'I'm still alive and you can go to blazes, whoever you are!' Then he hangs up."

"Oh, brother!" Carole threw back her head and laughed. "He certainly *is* going to be a hard nut to crack."

She saw Jon's gaze following her motions, lingering on her hair and face. For a moment he looked at her searchingly, as though something about her both baffled and intrigued him. Carole felt herself reddening beneath his scrutiny. Had she laughed too loudly? She was relieved when he drew his eyes away and started the car.

They drove high into the mountains where spruce, fir and hemlock trees crowded Jon's car. There were pine trees, too, laden with small black cones, and the air was fragrant with their tangy smell. The road took a sharp twist, curving still higher, and they passed sheer rock cliffs and a fantastic field of giant boulders.

"I should have come in the Bronco," Jon muttered.

A sudden sense of unease seized Carole as,

once again, her emotions grew ambivalent. They were traveling far off the beaten track, and she was all alone with Jon. After her experience with him several nights before she had been wary and now the same wariness returned. What if he chose to force himself on her? Would she be able to fight him—or would she even want to?

Without being aware of what she was doing, Carole edged closer toward the door on her side of the car.

"Relax." At the single dry word, she turned to look back at Jon. One of his black eyebrows lifted. "I won't attack you, Carole, even though I might like to. I promised to show you another side of myself, so that excludes bestial behavior. Whatever else I do, I keep my word!"

It was pointless to pretend that she hadn't experienced that moment's disquiet. "Sorry," Carole answered, her voice as dry as his.

At least he admitted that he'd like to have her in his arms. What was she to make of that?

Jon turned onto a lane so narrow that branches scraped the side of his car as it bounced over inhospitable ruts. "We're almost there," he said encouragingly.

"Pop Arnold certainly lives away from civilization, doesn't he?" Carole remarked, trying to steady herself against the impact of the sensations bombarding her.

"He's not overly fond of people," Jon informed her.

"I'll remember that," Carole said softly, wishing Jon's presence beside her was less disturbing and arousing.

The road dead-ended at a small clearing shadowed by vast mountains. A log cabin lay before them, puffs of smoke escaping from its chimney.

From around the side of the cabin two black-spotted dogs came, barking ferociously. One flung himself against Carole's side of the car, huge paws covering her window, angry red eyes staring at her. Despite her determination to be a resourceful, independent reporter, Carole quailed.

"Don't worry." She felt Jon's light touch on her shoulder. "They're not really vicious. I'll get out and quiet them down."

"Are you sure you're not risking an arm and a leg?" Carole said nervously.

"Well, let's see." Jon laughed at her.

He alighted and immediately sent the dogs slinking away with an earsplitting whistle. Grinning, he came over to open the door for Carole.

"They're well trained, at least," she said, relieved.

Around the side of the cabin came a bent old man with hair like snow and black baleful Haughton eyes. A rifle lay in the crook of his arm and without even realizing what she was doing, Carole gripped Jon's elbow.

He smiled down at her in momentary reassurance, then called to the bent, stooped figure. "Put down your shootin' iron, Pop; you've got company."

Once inside the woodsy little cabin, Carole sat at a huge round table that was obviously hand-hewn, her cassette recorder and notepad before her. Also before her was a steaming mug of the strongest, blackest coffee she'd ever seen. When she'd added her customary amount of cream, it disappeared into the blackness without a trace. Lavishly she added more, stirred in an exceptional amount of sugar as well, and took a cautious sip. The coffee was fresh and delicious.

Jon, seated across from her, had spent the last ten minutes informing Pop Arnold about the health and well-being of various family members that the old patriarch hadn't seen for some time. Easily Jon glided into a description of the project on which he and Carole were embarked.

To Carole's relief the fierce-looking old man with bushy white eyebrows had accepted her name and presence noncommittally. But when Jon fell silent at last, Pop Arnold turned to stare at her again.

"Yep, you're a Coldren girl," he said, identifying her as readily as Aunt Eugenia had Jon. "It's a marvel, in a way. Though Haughtons and Coldrens keep marrying into other families, they still keep on looking the same."

"A puzzle for some geneticist perhaps?" Jon said wryly.

The old man didn't find the word unfamiliar. In fact, as Carole looked at the all-wood book-cases crammed with volumes of all kinds, she knew the mountaineer in faded overalls was anything but illiterate.

"Might be," Pop Arnold conceded, pulling out a pipe and beginning to tamp down its contents. A match flared briefly and he puffed in silence for a few minutes. Then he looked back at his great-nephew with a harsh laugh.

"So you and Miss Coldren are working together on a history of the families and their feud. You know, I find that mighty interesting."

If he were interested, then surely he'd cooperate! Carole found herself gripping her coffee mug eagerly, but she knew enough to leave the conversation to Jon.

"Why not?" he said casually. "Seems like it's time for all of us to learn to live together in peace."

"Reckon so," the old man agreed through another puff on his pipe. Then his eyes narrowed above its stem. "This the same Coldren woman you were mixed up with ten—fifteen years ago?" he asked Jon abruptly.

Now it was Jon's turn to flush. Carole saw the color rising across his high cheekbones, staining the hollows beneath. "Yes," he said shortly. Clearly he disliked any and all references to his and Carole's shared past.

"Downright full of brotherly love, aren't you both?" Pop Arnold said, his tone arid.

"That's scarcely true." Jon's reply was frank and flat. "Matter of fact, a certain ingrained lack of trust is what keeps me checking up on Carole every step of the way."

"And I'm accompanying him to see all the

Haughtons so *he* can't pull a fast one," she said quietly.

"Thought so," the old man said in satisfaction.

An electric silence hung in the air. After a moment Carole felt obliged to break it. "Mr. Haughton, we really do need your help," she said urgently.

"I'll have to study on that a while," the old man remarked.

How long was a while? she wondered.

"It's not like I'd be telling a story about some stranger," Pop Arnold went on. "It's my own momma, Ellen Ann, you're wanting to know about. I've never discussed it. Never told a living soul.

"No, that's not quite right," he said, after a moment's reflection. "One reason I moved up here more than sixty years ago was people kept pestering me. News hounds. Nosy Parkers. Other Haughtons. One thing I told my wife the day I married her was, 'Don't ask me questions. Too many people are dead already. It's not to be mentioned.' Mary was a good woman. She did like I asked. And I never even told *her* till our kids were grown and we had grandchildren coming by to visit us on Sundays. Then, when I knew Mary was dying, I finally told her the story. She took it to the grave with her."

"Aunt Mary was a remarkable woman," Jon said quietly.

"She was." The old man continued to puff on his pipe. "Best thing any man can have is a good wife. Time you started thinking about that, Jon.

"Far as the other goes, let me study on it," he said again. "Writings have meant a lot of pleasure to me. We'll see about it."

He rose from the table, and Carole knew he considered the conversation effectively closed. But at least Pop Arnold hadn't said no.

The next couple of weeks were the most exciting Carole had known for years. Outwardly not all that much was happening, so when Carole was being honest with herself she knew it was because she spent most of those days with Jon. He was still the most fascinating man she'd ever met. Part of it was his tantalizing presence beside her in the car when she was close enough to catch the scent of him and enjoy the occasional smiles when his white teeth flashed. The other part was his conversation, whether she learned about what he'd been doing for the last several years or heard his comments on their project.

He had vacationed twice in Europe. "Between jobs I decided to treat myself to a little beauty and culture," he told her. "Maybe smooth off some of a mountain man's rough edges."

Privately Carole thought there weren't many of those rough edges. Jon had always been intelligent, perceptive and aware of the world beyond North Carolina. Eagerly she inquired as to where he'd gone.

"The first time I made the usual grand tour. Twenty countries in twenty-one days." He smiled. "The second time I rented a car and drove over the Continent and the British Isles, taking my time."

"Then you've been to Scotland?" she asked in surprise.

"Oh, yes. I trod the same bloody ground where the Haughtons and Coldrens used to square off at one another."

"Jon, your having been to Scotland may prove a tremendous asset," Carole said excitedly. "When I'm writing that portion you can help with descriptions of the countryside, the climate, the hills and sea."

"Good." He turned to regard her with his flashing dark eyes. "Haven't you ever been abroad?"

"Four marvelous days in London a few years ago," she replied. "Since then I've been too busy to travel much."

On another drive he suddenly broached a more emotion-charged subject. "Why haven't you ever married, Carole? A woman who looks like you has certainly been pursued."

After she recovered from her surprise at his personal question, Carole decided to answer as honestly as she could. "I've been engaged twice. Both my fiancés were fine men, but neither was that exactly right man. When I realized it, I broke off each engagement."

A small muscle moved beneath his smooth cheek. "Who were those men? What did they do?"

"Brian Howard was an advertising executive whom I met on my first job. David Mellor was an internist I was introduced to at a party. Now, what about you, Jon Haughton?" she asked, neatly turning the tables. "A man who looks like you has certainly been pursued, too."

"I've had a few close calls," he replied easily. He was being less candid than she, for he did not mention his late fiancée.

That ended their personal discussion, though Carole felt his speculative gaze on her several times during the course of that day.

During the remainder of the time, while they waited for Arnold Haughton's answer, they visited Aunt Eugenia again and listened to the Coldrens' version of Haughton duplicity during the American Civil War. They also worked occasionally in Carole's office at the library.

Sometimes, when she felt that old tug that seemed to draw her toward Jon, Carole had to pull back mentally and remind herself of several less-than-pleasant facts. This charming, companionable side of Jon was not his only side. She'd seen the darker one, and it had been too vivid to forget. Also, the reason Jon was here, poring carefully over her notes as she typed them, was to make sure she didn't delete anything that he considered pertinent to the story or insert anything damaging to his family. He was acting as watchdog, and that was a long way from the trust required for true collaboration.

Occasionally Tom Kaufman joined them for lunch or a visit at the library. His own contributions arose from long hours spent at the courthouse, perusing old records of land sales as well as those relating to marriages, births and deaths. Since many of those records were far from complete, he often requested that Carole and Jon check with various family members to learn whether Joe Haughton had left the county or simply disappeared from its rolls or whether Brady Coldren had ever married.

Yes, Carole found her days exciting. It was her evenings and weekends that left much to be desired, for after she and Jon had finished work for the day, he disappeared. Was he still seeing the attractive and winsome Lois Wyler? Carole wondered. That was certainly a logical assumption when she remembered the small white hand that Lois had dropped on Jon's arm. Also, on another occasion, she'd seen a box containing a toy in the back seat of Jon's car. Although he never mentioned it, Carole was sure it must have been a gift for Lois's children.

She spent the lackluster evenings watching television with Uncle Paul and Aunt Louise, washing her hair and doing her nails, or writing letters to her mother and various friends in Houston. One night she and Betsy went to a movie, and on another they all went to Susan and Reggie's house for dinner. The house was a modern ranch-style brick, and they were justifiably proud of it. Also, Susan proved to be quite a good cook, though she only nibbled at her own offerings.

Yet whenever she was around Susan and Reggie there was an uncomfortable atmosphere that filled Carole with unease. Why did Reggie wear such a hangdog look at the sight of Carole? Why was Susan so obviously nervous and fidgety, flinging out one question after another?

At least Carole now had some basis for suspecting the reason. Eleven years ago Susan, probably accompanied by Reggie, had gone to Uncle Buck Coldren and informed him that his Texas niece was sneaking around to meet Jon Haughton.

Even at this late date, Carole felt some indignation over Susan's obvious meddling, but what good would it do to rehash it now? Susan must have acted out of good intentions, and if Jon had truly loved Carole, he would not have allowed Buck to scare him away. Still, Carole found herself fielding Susan's present-day questions warily.

"We were certainly surprised to find that Jon has been driving you around," Susan said in the kitchen when Carole helped her wash up after their meal. "Are you two getting involved again?"

"Oh, no," Carole said, striving for a bright tone. "It's strictly business between us."

"Doesn't he ever talk about the past?" Susan persisted.

"No, he doesn't like that topic of conversation," Carole replied briefly.

"You mean he hasn't said *anything*?" Susan went on doggedly and, Carole thought, guiltily.

"Good heavens, what's to say?" Carole asked. "He dropped me, that's all. I hear that later he was engaged to a girl he truly loved, but unfortunately she died. I'm sure he'd find any explanations awkward."

"Oh," said Susan flatly.

A warning bell chimed in Carole's mind. "Why do you ask, Susan?" she asked curiously. "Is there something I should know?"

"Oh, no!" Susan looked taken aback. "I'm just interested, that's all."

At least that put an end to that particular topic. Over coffee and cake Reggie inquired about what Carole had learned from the family interviews so far.

Carole was frankly glad that Tom Kaufman had introduced this subject—the natural curiosity of both families—during the last luncheon she and Jon had shared with him.

"You're both going to hear a lot of questions," he advised, "and it's my opinion that you should tell people to wait until they can read the book. Otherwise, both families are going to be gossiping about what Auntie-This supposedly said or Cousin-That's story. Anything taken out of context can be badly misconstrued."

Carole and Jon had both nodded, knowing this to be sage advice. Now Carole tried to explain that to her curious kinfolk. They reacted with silence and hurt feelings.

Carole was very glad when the evening ended and she could retreat to the quiet of her familiar upstairs bedroom. Yet even there peace eluded her. When she came back from the bathroom, having cleaned her face in preparation for sleep, she passed Betsy's door and heard her cousin's voice within. Automatically Carole's eyes went to the telephone table that stood in the upstairs hallway, holding the phone that she and Betsy shared. The instrument was gone, its cord stretched into the girl's bedroom so that her late night conversation could not be overheard.

To whom was she talking? Carole wondered a trifle grimly, hearing the low hum of inaudible words. Then, realizing that she must not infringe on the girl's privacy, Carole walked on to her own room and closed the door.

Please don't let it be Terry Rodgers! Carole found herself praying. A teenage romance could be so intense . . . and so painful when it didn't work out. Carole sat on the edge of her bed, remembering how ghastly her last year of high school had been when she was back in Houston and knew Jon had forsaken her. For months she had suffered such pains in her chest and stomach that she could scarcely breathe, eat or concentrate on her studies.

It had taken Carole more than a year to pull out of her severe depression. In fact, it was not until she was in college at the University of Texas that she'd finally started to perk up a bit. College men began noticing her, and Carole, realizing that she couldn't pine forever over a memory, had forced herself to resume dating.

But her initial experience with love had set a disastrous pattern for the future, and Carole found that none of her subsequent romances worked out, either. Although she found a career that interested her and for which she had a natural flair, Carole also yearned for marriage and motherhood. Out of those yearnings and the pressure of the passing years, she had twice attempted to compromise with love.

Her engagement to Brian had ended precipitously. Carole had accompanied him on a skiing trip to Aspen. There, in a rented condo on a slope of the Rockies, she looked first at the king-size bed which she was expected to share at last with Brian, then at the man himself. She saw a sleek, good-looking ad executive who was a complete stranger to her heart. Carole told him that they'd made a mistake and flew back home, leaving Brian to ski alone. He recovered quickly, for a year later Carole had heard that he was married.

With David it had been a sadder story. He was a deserving young physician, and Carole had thought that surely this time things would work out. She was full of hope when she accepted the small yet tasteful solitaire he pressed on her. But that relationship, too, had ended as she tried to explain to David that it was all her fault, not his, that she couldn't love him.

No words of hers had been able to soothe his wounded spirit and bruised male ego. At first, David continued to try to woo and win her. When he gave up at last, he had grown bitter. Thinking of him then, Carole found herself hoping that David was not bitter still. But he had never married, and mutual friends reported that he'd had little to do with women since.

Her own terrible hurt had led Carole to unintentionally hurt others. Now, when she was concerned about her cousin, Carole realized that as never before.

Troubled, she crawled into her narrow bed, and eventually sleep came to rescue her.

"Telephone for you, Carole."

Betsy's sleepy voice jerked Carole awake shortly after dawn the next morning. "Oh!" she cried, springing up. She thrust her feet into slippers and padded out into the hall in her pajamas.

Betsy stood there wearing a long, old-fashioned nightgown, the phone receiver clutched in her hand. Despite the early hour and the fact that she, too, was barely awake, the girl's cheeks were bright with excitement.

"I think it's *him*," she whispered to Carole, handing over the phone.

"Tom Kaufman?" Carole asked. He was the man who phoned her most frequently.

"No! It's that good-looking Mr. Haughton."

Carole awoke completely on the spot. Her heartbeat accelerated as she reached to take the phone from Betsy. "Hello?"

"Tell your little cousin that I appreciate her comment," Jon said, merriment in his voice.

"Oh, you heard that? Well, you must realize she's young and impressionable," Carole replied, watching the door to Betsy's room close behind the girl.

"Still, she has taste," Jon teased, "though I suppose not everyone would agree."

I would agree, Carole thought silently.

"What I'm calling about at this very early hour is that I've heard from Pop Arnold," Jon went on, his voice growing more serious. "He's an early riser. At four-thirty or five this morning, some god-awful time like that, he called."

"Yes?" Carole said excitedly, gripping the telephone.

"He said he'd decided against telling us about the old feud. He didn't think it would be wise. That certain happenings are best forgotten. I believe that's an accurate summation of his statement."

"Oh." Carole was so stunned that she could barely utter the word. A stinging sense of disappointment whipped over her.

"Cheer up," Jon said, gauging Carole's tone accurately. "As my mother always told me, you have to judge people not by what they say but by what they do."

"What do you mean?" Carole said, a single spark of hope rising anew.

"I mean that when a man like Pop Arnold, who hates telephones and never calls anyone, phones me before dawn he's very interested no matter what he says. So throw on your clothes, pretty gal, and let's go see him again. All he needs is a little support and encouragement!"

Chapter Seven

*L*ess than an hour later Carole and Jon were riding down the highway, sharing a box of doughnuts and passing a pint bottle of orange juice back and forth. Jon had picked up their breakfast at a local diner while Carole was hurriedly throwing on jeans and a plaid shirt.

Her grooming had been swift. She'd washed her face, brushed her teeth and hair and added a touch of lip gloss. Then she'd snatched up her cassette recorder and waited, yawning, on the front porch for Jon.

He arrived in the large tan Bronco, wearing jeans that hugged his lean hips and muscular thighs, a long-sleeved denim shirt and boots. Carole found it strangely exciting, almost erotic, to be drinking from the same side of the orange juice bottle. There was something so intimate in the sharing that she darted a quick glance at Jon. His profile, seen in repose, was dashingly handsome, and she noted that despite his obvious haste he had still taken time to shave.

She drank in the scents surrounding him. His breath, when he turned to speak to her, was still minty-morning fresh. She smelled his spicy aftershave, the clean aroma of a starched shirt and the rugged fragrance of leather.

"More orange juice?" Carole offered, trying to stop her thoughts of how his black hair grew down toward the nape of his neck. Her hands longed to explore his face, and when she looked at his lips she remembered how they could linger and cling to hers with surprising softness.

"No, what I really want is coffee, but I know Pop Arnold will provide plenty of that."

Jon was right. An hour later, when they were seated in Arnold Haughton's cabin once again, he served thick mugs filled with his inky, delicious coffee.

The old man was indeed ready to talk, his earlier words to his great-nephew to the contrary. After Carole and Jon had been their most charmingly persuasive, and Pop Arnold had hemmed and hawed a bit, he allowed Carole to turn on the cassette recorder.

Pop Arnold set down his pipe and began slowly. "You've got to know how it was with mountainfolk about a hundred years ago to understand my momma and poppa. Life here was hard. There was scarcely any contact with the world beyond. We were isolated, and what we couldn't grow or make or trade, we plain did without.

"My poppa was a hard man. Guess he had to be. He didn't marry till he was close to forty 'cause he couldn't afford a wife till then. When he finally went looking, one of his cousins had a bunch of half-grown, half-starved kids. He practically begged Cyrus, my poppa, to take Ellen Ann off his hands. My momma was about fourteen or fifteen, I reckon.

"She didn't want to marry Cyrus. I guess he looked powerfully old to her, but she didn't have a choice. She told me about it when I was four. I didn't understand then, of course, but I remembered her words.

"I don't think Poppa meant to be mean to her. Actually, when I study on it, I think he loved her, but the love got all twisted up with hate 'cause she hated him so. Little as I was, I knew she loved me and hated him. It was a mighty cold household for a little boy with those two never talking to each other lest they had to.

"Folks said it was a fair where my momma first saw Lucas Coldren. Guess that was right—I don't remember. I was probably asleep in the back of the wagon.

"What I do remember happened later that autumn. The trees were all yellow and orange and gold. My momma had gone down to the stream that ran back behind our cabin to wash some clothes. I was playing in the shallow water when there was a rustling in the brush and this big tall man stepped out.

"At first I was scared of him," Arnold Haughton related, "even though he smiled at me, 'cause momma acted like she was scared. She called out, 'You shouldn't have come here, Lucas Coldren!'

"The tall man just looked at her. He had hair

like the autumn—kind of like yours, Carole—all streaked with yellow and gold. 'I had to come, Ellen Ann,' he told her. 'I've tried to forget you, but I can't.'

"Momma started crying and she ran over to him, and they put their arms around each other. I remember I thought it was funny for two grown people to stand there hugging and kissing like that. Then I heard him say, 'I'm going to take you away, Ellen Ann. We'll go to Texas—I've heard it's mighty fine there.'

"Momma kept hanging onto him like he'd offered her heaven. Then she pointed to me. 'What about my boy?' she said. 'I'm not leaving my boy.'

"I'll always remember what Luke Coldren said then. 'What belongs to you, Ellen Ann, belongs to me. I'll be good to your boy.'

"They talked so much about Texas," the old man said, then paused for a puff on his pipe. "I thought about that this week, how often I heard those two talk about going to Texas—and now Carole's turned up and she's from Texas. Seemed like a strange coincidence. Maybe even a sign."

Carole nodded wordlessly, afraid to break the spell the old man was weaving.

"Why didn't they leave?" Jon asked softly.

"Weather," the old man said succinctly. "It was autumn that day by the stream. That night there came an early snowfall, and next morning it was winter. We were all snowed in.

"I sure remember that winter," he went on. "It was harsh and cold. Poppa was gone a lot, hunting meat for the winter and setting traps for furs. Whenever Momma thought it was safe, she'd bundle me up and we'd go rushing down to the stream. Luke was usually waiting there. Wonder he didn't freeze to death! He'd have an extra horse for Momma, and he'd put me in the saddle in front of him and take us to his cabin.

"It looked about the same as ours 'cept we were all happy there. Luke and Momma would laugh and talk." With a sigh, the old man stopped. "Guess I'd better tell the whole story if I'm going to tell any of it. I know they shared more than talk and kisses. Not that *I* ever saw what went on in the loft upstairs! But I knew there was something exciting and secret. Again and again, both Momma and Luke made me promise I'd never tell Poppa. I didn't, of course. I loved them and I was scared of him.

"'Early winter and a late thaw,'" he quoted. "That's what folks say in these parts. It was true that year. My, but those two were wild to get away. Sometimes Momma cried and said, 'Won't it *ever* quit snowing?' I guess I know the reason she got cabin fever. She found out she was going to have a baby. I remember Luke putting his hand on her stomach, remember him promising her, 'We'll get away before anyone finds out.'

"Finally, the snow started melting, and one morning Poppa told Momma he was going off to trade mink and bearskins. He wasn't going to the settlement at Green Grove but on to Asheville, where he'd heard prices were better. He planned to be gone about two weeks."

The old man stopped to sip more coffee, and Carole saw that white spots had appeared at the corners of his wrinkled lips. Quietly Jon got up and brought the coffeepot, refilling the old man's cup.

"Once Poppa had ridden off with his furs, you never saw such a happy woman as Momma. She fixed a knapsack to hold a few of our clothes, then she rushed me out of the cabin. She kept saying, 'Arnold, we're going to Texas!'

"Luke hadn't known there was a chance of us coming that day, so it was 'bout the only time I recall when he wasn't waiting by the stream. We had to walk to his cabin and that was an awful far piece for a little boy.

"It was mid-afternoon by the time we got there. My, Luke was glad to see us! But I was so plumb tuckered out all I wanted to do was eat and sleep. On account of me, they decided they'd better wait till morning to leave.

"They should have gone right away," the old man said flatly, "but they thought they were safe at last. So Momma fixed me some milktoast and bedded me down by the fire, then she and Luke started packing up his wagon."

Another long silence fell, but neither Carole nor Jon stirred, afraid to break the flow of the old man's memories.

"I've thought on it for years," Arnold Haughton went on after a moment. "Wondering if there was any way they could have escaped. Maybe if they'd left right after Momma and I arrived and not bothered with the wagon, just traveled by horseback . . ."

"I doubt it," Jon said gently. "I'm sure he was watching for them."

"I think so, too." Pop Arnold nodded over his pipe.

"Who?" Carole asked, then comprehension dawned. "You mean Ellen Ann's husband?"

Jon shrugged. "Who else, Carole? You called him the likeliest suspect on that first tape with your Aunt Eugenia. He set a trap and let Ellen Ann and Luke walk right into it. Maybe he didn't know for sure what they were planning. He just had his suspicions and wanted to make sure."

"He made sure." Arnold Haughton's voice stirred with remembered emotions. "Just 'bout an hour after midnight, when he knew we'd likely all be asleep, he burst into the cabin. At the racket, Luke came running down from the loft. He saw Poppa and he turned to grab his rifle off the wall. Poppa fired then and Luke went down, shot through the back of his skull. Momma ran to Luke. When she saw he was dead, she looked like she'd died, too. She looked up at Poppa and she wasn't even scared. 'Shoot me, too,' she told him, ''cause I don't want to live without Luke.'" Dryly, Arnold said, "He obliged her."

"And you saw it all?" Carole said to Pop Arnold, horrified for the frightened little boy he'd once been.

He nodded and drew on the stem of his pipe. "'Course I was in shock, that's what they'd call it now. I did just what Poppa told me to do, which was lie back down again. He took the bodies, one by one, and came back for me just about dawn. Then we left for Asheville."

"That trip was his alibi," Jon interjected.

"Yep. You know, I still don't remember a thing about it," Pop Arnold confided, "except that in Asheville Poppa bought me a bag of candy that tasted mighty good. After that, I kind of came to myself, but I was as lonesome and scared as any kid ever was. 'Course Poppa was talking to me all the time, like Momma and Luke had earlier, warning me I mustn't ever tell what I'd seen and heard. He didn't have to worry. I never talked much to anybody about anything. I didn't have a lot of use for people after that."

Carole's heart thumped with grief at the sad old tale. "What happened to that wretched man who was your father?" she whispered.

"He married again a couple of years later," Pop Arnold said with a sigh. "Had three more young'uns. Then, when he was past sixty, he 'went queer.' That's what folks called it in those days when a man started acting crazy. One night I guess the demons got too much for him. He took his rifle and went outside. He set it on the ground and used his big toe to pull the trigger. He blew his brains out.

"That's all I've got to say 'cept for one thing," Arnold Haughton added in summation. "Though the Coldrens weren't guilty of the murders, they were just as bent on revenge as the Haughtons, and revenge never solves anything. So I think both families were equally wrong. There is divine justice, if people just trust in it. But I never heard of either a Coldren or a Haughton turning the other cheek . . . 'cept maybe once." He cast an oblique look at Jon.

Jon reached across the table and wordlessly gripped the old man's hand. Carole reached for his other hand and gave it a comforting squeeze.

"Now—" With a little shake, as though to throw off the past, Pop Arnold arose and went to get his coffeepot. "Seems like there's new trouble brewing between the families again."

If he had dropped a bomb, they couldn't have been more surprised.

"What?" Jon said. "I haven't heard a thing!"

Anxiously Carole looked across at him. "Me either," she said.

"Jeb Haughton's boy, Lon, stopped by here yesterday. He said Terry was in a spot of trouble. When I asked Lon what he meant, he said Terry was begging for it, messing with the Coldrens."

Jon's face darkened. "I knew Terry seemed preoccupied lately. I asked him about it, but he wouldn't say anything."

"Silence seems to be a characteristic of your family," Carole said over the ominous thumping of her heart.

Jon shot her a swift glance. "Maybe so," he agreed shortly. "Anyway, I'll get to the bottom of it. You can both be sure of that!"

Jon refused another cup of coffee, and Carole

retrieved her cassette recorder. After bidding the lonely old man good-bye, they were soon back in the Bronco.

Carole's mind was flooded with thoughts and feelings, both about the ancient story they'd just heard and the present-day concern about trouble between the youngsters of Green Grove. Was Betsy mixed up in this? Did she know anything about it? Carole thought in alarm. Her instinctive reaction was to protect the girl.

They had driven several miles before Jon spoke. "Carole, are you sure—really sure—that you've heard nothing about any new trouble?"

Carole was startled that his thoughts so closely paralleled her own. "Jon, I swear I haven't heard a thing!"

Should she divulge her suspicions? she wondered. That was all she had, just vague unfounded suspicions.

"There's a sheriff's car following us right now," he said.

"What?" Carole gasped. Before she could swivel her head to look, Jon caught her arm in a hard clasp. "No, don't turn around. We don't want them to be aware that we've noticed them."

"Who is it?" she whispered, dry-mouthed and terrified. How strange to feel afraid of people who were her kin, like Uncle Buck or her various cousins who served as deputies.

"I can't see who it is." Jon's reply was terse. Then, after a moment, his grip on Carole's arm relaxed. Quietly he said, "It's all right. False alarm. The car has turned off."

Carole waited for relief to flood her and felt despair instead. "This damned feud!" she said hoarsely. "Will it never, ever end!" To her surprise, her words ended on a sob.

She didn't burst into tears; her grief wasn't that simple. Rather, her body shook uncontrollably while great tears rolled hotly down her face. Carole put both hands to her cheeks to wipe the tears away, but others fell even faster.

With a wordless exclamation, Jon pulled the truck off the road and beneath the shelter of a great spreading tree. With the engine still running, he turned and pulled Carole into his arms.

Now she felt relief; now with his arms holding her lightly she felt a blessed balm spread over her troubled mind and soul. Gratefully she buried her face in his strong chest, while her tears stopped as quickly as they had begun.

Oh, how good he felt! How wonderful to feel him patting her back soothingly. Gratefully Carole drank in the wonderful sensations of his skin on hers. His smooth-shaven cheek resting on hers, his fingers tangling in her hair, and the touch of something so warm and comforting brushing her forehead. His lips? she wondered.

"Oh, Jon, I would do anything—anything!—to see this terrible feud over and done with!" she cried passionately.

"So would I, Carole," he whispered against her forehead.

She lifted her face to look up at him and found her lips poised just inches from his. Slowly his head bent down.

He kissed her as he first had so long ago, on that Fourth of July when they had met, his lips barely brushing hers. Then the fire that always sprang up between them ignited anew, this time in tender longing.

Jon's lips pressed more deeply on Carole's, then moved away to brush her cheeks, her forehead, her throat. While all her senses came wildly, clamoringly alive, she heard the rapid intake of his breath. His lips returned to hers with greater fire and urgency than before.

Carole could only cling to him, answering his burning yet tender kisses. Her arms wound around his back, to move up and down the strong broad expanse presented there. Her eager fingers ran from Jon's shoulder blades to just below his armpits and down to where the sinewy flesh narrowed at his waist. How safe she felt, hugged so tightly against him, sheltered by his arms.

His lips continued to burn on hers, and with their deepening pressure Carole felt the weight of her breasts tingling and knew that her nipples were hard as diamonds.

Jon drew her closer, to lie across his lap, and she could feel the force of his desire. Suddenly her whole body throbbed with longing.

Her hands dropped to his thighs and lightly traced the muscles there. She heard him suck in his breath and knew that even her feathery touch had enflamed him further.

Carole wanted to sink and drown in his embrace—yearned to know him in the deepest, most secret recess of her body. She felt powerless to resist the deep, hot tide of feeling sweeping over her, yet perversely she felt powerful, too, as she never had before. It was a purely feminine power that gloried in Jon's answering response and desire.

His hands, moving warmly and rapidly, began unbuttoning her shirt, and Carole moaned softly against his exciting lips. With his touch evoking delicious tingles, Jon's hands glided over the satiny skin of her rib cage and rose to stroke her breasts, so lightly constrained by a filmy bra.

Carole felt a fiery excitement sweeping over her. "Jon . . . oh, Jon," she whispered. Her own hands moved instinctively, caressing his knees, then gliding back up the lean, tension-gripped thighs.

He gasped at her touch, and his fingers slipped warmly behind her bra. For a moment he fumbled with its hook, then her breasts were freed from all confinement. Jon's hands slid upward, delighting in the feeling of her skin, teasing the taut nipples that tightened even further at his silent adoration. His black head bent down to tease and encircle a pink tip, then he sucked softly at the upthrust mound. Carole stroked his head as it lay there, while passion surged through her in such primitive, overwhelming waves that her whole body quaked and trembled.

His tongue flashed to lave her other nipple, trailing almost unbearable excitement in its wake. Then his mouth fastened there as well. Carole heard her breath coming heavily, desirously, as she longed from the depths of her soul to belong wholly to him. Her body clamored for the ultimate fulfillment of his.

He raised his head to look into her eyes, his own cloudy with need, yet darkly somber from—*what*? For the first time since she'd felt his arms closing around her, Carole was aware of something besides the melting and yearning of her senses.

Jon's eyes cleared, lit now by something that was certainly concern and might even have been fear. The stark look between them lengthened, while, suddenly and simultaneously, both sets of stroking hands stilled. Sanity had returned.

"Now you'll think I'm not a man of my word," Jon said, drawing away. His voice was husky, yet it cooled rapidly. "My apologies, Carole. You're a very beautiful woman—as I'm sure you've been told."

That certainly sounded like the new and cynical side of Jon! "No apology necessary," Carole said tightly and turned away from him to fasten her bra, then button her shirt. Her fingers still shook from desire. "Whatever happened here was obviously unplanned and—and mutual."

"You're a remarkably honest person." Jon's

eyes held grudging respect as he turned his attention back to the still-running Bronco. "Actually, all I meant to do was offer you a shoulder to cry on."

"I appreciated the gesture." Although Carole tried to keep her voice light, a torrent still raged within her. Half of her felt relief when the vehicle pulled back onto the road while the other half clamored, wanting him, needing him, loving him.

Yes, *loving* him. Her eyes dewed with a fresh hot rush of tears as Carole faced the truth. She realized now that she still loved the tender, passionate Jon. She had always loved him. But that didn't change certain facts. The unpleasant truth was that Jon had abandoned her once, and there was no reason on earth to think he might not do it again.

No matter how much she loved him, Carole knew that she must hang on to her pride and keep her emotions under control. Disaster awaited her otherwise.

"Carole, dear, I hope you're being careful around that man," warned Wynne Coldren Marsh.

"If you mean Jon, then the answer is, yes, I'm being careful, Wynne," Carole replied, keeping her voice level.

"He led you astray once, my dear." Wynne tapped her cigarette in an ashtray and regarded Carole through a gray stream of smoke. "Jon Haughton is devious, immoral and unscrupulous . . . as any number of unfortunate women could tell you. Why, he's had ever so many disgusting affairs!"

And you still sound like the same jealous cat you've always been! Carole thought savagely. Afraid that her feelings might be written on her face, she turned and walked to the picture window in the apartment of her thrice-divorced cousin. She turned her back deliberately on Wynne and gazed out at the strong, beautiful, peaceful mountains.

She was really beginning to hate these family get-togethers, Carole admitted to herself. Each one seemed more unpleasant than the last. Behind her, Wynne continued to hiss her venomous stories of first one woman and then another who had pursued the handsome engineer.

The worst part, Carole thought drearily, was that some of what Wynne was so gleefully relating was probably true.

This was a "hen party" at Wynne's on a lazy Sunday afternoon. Carole had anticipated it with dread, and she could now be glad only that the meeting was fast drawing to a close. The other women—Susan, Jean and Connie, as well as Blake Coldren's wife Yvonne—were seated on the patio watching the sunset while they gossiped over a final Tom Collins. When Carole had excused herself to visit the kitchen for a glass of plain cold water, Cousin Wynne had come along to "help." The help was designed to enlighten Carole.

Carole needed no enlightening. She already

knew both the best and the worst of Jon Haughton. And despite everything she knew, or what anyone might choose to tell her, her heart ached because she loved him so. In spite of everything, she loved him.

At least she'd had little time to dwell on this now-recognized source of misery, for they had been very busy in the last several days.

Most of their efforts had involved tracking down various Coldren and Haughton members to try to verify the myriad stories that had been passed down from one generation to another. Despite some obvious animosity on the part of certain relatives, everyone proved quite eager to talk. Each had a repertoire of stories learned from long-dead grandparents, maiden aunts and distant cousins. There had been family Bibles to skim for vital statistics and a heartbreakingly long list of untimely deaths to compile.

Carole and Jon had also gone to see Aunt Eugenia for a final interview. That had been the worst of all, Carole decided in retrospect, for the old lady had described in technicolor detail the sights and sounds of the massacre by the Hilamunga River. She repeated the vicious shouted taunts and the unforgivable insults hurled back and forth across the water, ending when the sound of gunfire rang out. Then came the barrage of bullets when the ancient hills echoed and reverberated with sounds of war, curses and sobs. In less than two hours twenty-one people had been killed and the Hilamunga River ran red with blood.

The preacher had finally ended the carnage, riding boldly into the blood-red river to curse both families for their godless heathen ways. Finally the survivors, shamed and stunned, slunk away carrying their wounded. Then the women of both families came weeping to the river to collect their dead.

Both Carole and Jon were shaken by the story that left the decrepit old woman trembling in her chair. "Now, I've told it all," Aunt Eugenia said with finality. "God willing, I can finally forget it!" Quietly they had thanked her and left.

"It must never happen again," Jon said grimly when he opened the car door for Carole.

His words made her think anew of the disturbing rumors of present-day trouble. "Jon, what have you found out from Terry?" she said anxiously.

"Nothing," he said, his voice defeated. "Either that kid is a champion liar, or Lon was just shooting off his mouth, as he often does."

Carole hoped Jon was right, but the unease that she had felt in the pit of her stomach stirred once again.

On all their recent days together, Jon had acted the perfect gentleman and ideal chauffeur, driving Carole back to her library office when their work was done. Carole, seated beside him, had longed for the comfort of his arms and the abandon of his embrace. His long, strong body next to hers was a constant source of temptation and frustration. But Jon hadn't made another move toward her, although from the way his eyes sometimes turned smoky and he drew a deep breath, Carole was sure he battled desires every bit as strong as her own. She yearned for a break in his rigid control.

That constant awareness of each other's presence was always between them, like a barely banked fire, ready at any moment to flame into life.

At least she would see him tomorrow, Carole thought, turning back from the picture window to confront Cousin Wynne's vindictive face. This had been such a long, empty weekend—the worst one yet—but at least Jon had promised to call her early Monday morning.

"I thought of something yesterday, Carole."

Jon's promised call began with that announcement. "I remembered how many old abandoned cabins still exist, scattered here and there throughout the mountains. So I called Pop Arnold and, for once, he was willing to talk on the phone. He said that the cabin Lucas Coldren had built was still standing, though it's in a sorry state. When he described its location I remembered it vaguely from times when I went deer hunting as a kid with my brother Robert and our Indian friend, Willie Running-Brook. Robert said it was haunted, and Willie claimed to feel the presence of evil spirits. Since they scared the daylights out of me, I still remember the cabin's exact location. Would you like to go take a look at it?"

Carole hesitated for a moment. The thought of

viewing the old cabin where Luke and Ellen Ann had died was not a very appealing one, but, as a writer, Carole knew she ought to go. Also, there was the chance to be alone with Jon for a few precious hours, and while that might be dangerous, it was also too alluring to resist.

"Yes! Yes, I do," she said decisively.

"O.K. We'll have to walk in and out, and that will take most of the day. Dress for outdoors. Jeans and high boots, if you've got 'em. It's tough to see snakes in all that underbrush."

Carole shuddered, but having made her decision, she was not about to be deterred.

She put on her oldest clothes for the trek: faded skin-tight jeans that she'd planned to wear only around the house; a long-sleeved Western shirt of red cotton; her sturdy yet expensive hand-tooled Texas boots.

Carole told Aunt Louise that she would be gone all day and accepted her aunt's help in making several thick sandwiches stuffed liberally with ham and cheese.

Less than an hour later Jon rolled up in the Bronco, and Carole saw approval on his face, both for her attire and the brown sack lunch.

"I brought a few things, too," he said as Carole leaped agilely into the high vehicle. "Coffee. Mosquito and tick spray. Cookies and candy."

"What? No snake-bite kit?" she couldn't resist asking.

"Of course," he said, and his nonchalance horrified her all over again. "I also brought my pistol."

Later, high up in the thickly forested mountains, Carole watched with some awe as Jon strapped the pistol over his jeans. "You really think we might see snakes?" she asked nervously.

"Snakes, wild boars, black bears . . . you never can tell. Hey, don't look so scared," he jibed as though he could hear the chattering of Carole's teeth. "I'll go first and lead the way."

After the first fifteen minutes, when Carole's every step was taken fearfully, she began to relax and enjoy the walk. It was the perfect day for an outing such as this, and she marveled at the thick woods and myriad plants. Mosses and wood ferns, flowering shrubs and wild orchids— all stirred her to delight. The sun streaked through the thick trees, guiding them along an old, almost overgrown footpath. As she hurried behind Jon, Carole thought of Ellen Ann and Luke. Had they trod this very path when they hurried to their clandestine meetings?

The path rose higher and grew narrower, winding through the massive woods, and before long all direct sunlight was obliterated by the great stands of trees. The filtered light grew misty green. Except for beetles' clicks, frogs' croaks and their own muffled footsteps, the forest was eerily quiet.

Then they emerged into a small clearing where bright sun slanted down. Carole was glad when they came upon a small stream trickling over gray boulders and Jon called a halt. They bent down by the stream to drink deeply of its clear, icy cold water and wash their hands and faces. Then they unpacked their lunch. Carole, relaxing with a sandwich beneath the shade of a tree, was reminded of the day when she and Jon had first met. She wondered if similar thoughts ever occurred to him, and she watched him covertly from behind the screen of her eyelashes. He fit so naturally here in this setting. A light wind ruffled his thick dark hair, blowing it across his forehead. Carole felt the desire to reach out and smooth it back. Felt the urge to run her fingers across his face. How she wished he would reach out for her, touch her, hold her.

Evidently Jon wasn't receiving those particular signals, for he soon sprang to his feet and extended a strong hand to help Carole up. "Let's go," he said and added encouragingly, "it's not much farther."

Another twenty minutes of walking, much of it uphill, brought them to the top of a large peak. At first glance it appeared much like any other, the wilderness having reclaimed what had once been a homestead, but Jon pointed out the signs of previous habitation. Rotting chunks of wood marked a fallen split-rail fence. An ancient wagon wheel lay rusting in the grass. There were stones in evidence, too, from a collapsed chimney.

They stepped between an alley of trees, and Carole caught her breath at the first glimpse of the old cabin. Gray and weather-beaten, most of its roof was gone, leaving it open to the elements. Brambles and thick underbrush made their approach to it cautious and slow.

Jon stepped warily up onto the narrow porch, then pushed aside a heavy half-ajar door. He reached a hand back for Carole. She clutched at it as though it were her lifeline.

The interior of the small cabin was empty of furniture and cooking utensils. It had been raided years before of all useful items, Jon explained quietly to Carole.

She glanced around and saw the cold hearth. The mantel above it was still intact. Had Luke Coldren once leaned against that, as Jon had leaned against his own mantel? Had Ellen Ann bent down to warm her hands at the hearth? Somewhere by the fire the little boy who had once been Pop Arnold had slept while the lovers shared their passionate kisses.

What remained of the disintegrating plank floor was stained from rain and snow, but Carole, picking her way across it, knew blood had been spilled here. The blood of two people who had dreamed of a new life in Texas but were unable to escape the fury of the feud and the repercussions of their love for each other.

Suddenly a small mammal, about the size of a kitten, scurried out from a hiding place and scooted across the rotting floor. It ran over the toe of Carole's left boot and only then did she recognize it. "A rat!" she screamed.

The next thing she knew, she was in Jon's arms where she'd flung herself, clutching him with all her strength while her heart rocked her with its frantic pounding. "My God, Jon, did you see the *size* of that rat?" she said, half-sobbing as she shivered against his firm chest.

"Let's get out of here," he said swiftly. "We've seen enough."

He led her back outside while she continued to clutch at him with frenzied fingers.

"My goodness, Carole!" He laughed down at her as they stood again in the dappled sunlight. "If I didn't know any better, I'd say you were scared of rats."

"I'm scared of rats, snakes, bats. . . ." She squeezed her eyes tightly shut, trying to erase the memory of the furry gray creature that had frightened her so.

"It's all right," Jon said consolingly. "It's O.K., sweetheart."

Her ears registered the careless endearment. She knew he probably meant nothing by it, yet the mere fact of his having said it mattered to Carole. Tremulously she raised her lips to his. "Oh, Jon, hold me!" she whispered.

"Carole!" His strong arms wrapped around her, and then his lips came down bruisingly on hers.

She didn't care that his arms almost cut off her breath or that his mouth plundered hers remorselessly. She clung to him in rapture, knowing that Jon was not trying to hurt her now but rather was gripped by a desire as fierce and intense as her own.

His mouth left a trail of burning kisses across

her face. For a moment he buried his face against her throat, rubbing the soft skin there not only with his lips but with his chin, nose and cheek, as though he could absorb her through such a rich and total touch. Then his mouth covered hers again, hot and sweet and filled with hunger.

Carole answered his kiss, forgetting everything but the wonderful, exhilarating sensations sweeping over her. Her back arched toward him, thrusting her breasts up, while her own hands ran eagerly over his shoulders and back.

Jon caught her closer, grinding his body against hers until Carole could feel the buttons of his shirt pushing into her chest, yet even that proved pleasurable.

Carole felt her hands rising to dig into his scalp, molding his mouth to hers. Like twin flames their lips sought, meshed with and savored each other's. The sweet, heated breath Carole gasped into her hungry lungs had come straight from his own, and with the realization of that sharing, her emotions swirled chaotically.

Beneath Jon's insistent lips Carole felt her mouth open, receptive. His tongue glided seductively into the inviting temple, its texture rough, yet tender in its movements. Her own tongue rose to meet his, to tickle and tease, entwine and caress.

Again Jon's body rubbed insinuatingly against hers, making Carole well aware of the need that churned through him. In the most intimate, feminine part of her body came an answering need—a hungry, gnawing aching.

She longed to give herself to him—here, now, in the bright sunlight and whispering glade of grass. Behind them lay a cabin of death, and, standing almost within its shadow, Carole wished for an affirmation of life—for the very act that gave life. Surely Jon could tell how she felt from her frenzied response to him.

The last thing she expected was for Jon to suddenly wrench his mouth from hers, breaking their embrace. When he did, Carole gave a small cry of disappointment. "Let's start back," he said, his voice husky yet abrupt. "We have quite a ways to go."

She followed after him blindly, her disappointment too crushing to allow her to care about the long walk back or anything else. At least the way seemed easier, since it was mostly downhill, but as Carole stumbled along on the old path her emotions were in turmoil. If only he had held her a moment longer, touched her more ardently, even borne her to the ground in an impetuous embrace! Her body throbbed with frustrated yearning.

This time they didn't pause beside the silver stream. Neither spoke during the rest of their hike back to the Bronco, and it didn't seem long until they were moving down the road again. The wind rushing in through Carole's open window cooled her flushed face but did nothing toward dissipating the heat of her body. She stole a glance at Jon as he drove, and he looked cold, stern and very much in control. At least he didn't appear to be gloating over Carole's having thrown herself at him. But she felt the humiliation of that moment back by the old cabin and her soul writhed. Never before had she begged a man to hold her and cried out with dismay when he released her too soon.

Tree shadows were lengthening, and mist had gathered again to cloak the mountains when they reached the outskirts of Green Grove. "Did you tell your folks you'd be late?" Jon asked, taking his eyes off the road for the very first time to look at Carole.

"Yes," she said defiantly, wondering why he had asked.

"Let's stop by my place for a drink. There appears to be a rather pressing personal matter that we need to resolve."

Oh, God, he sounded like a schoolteacher! Carole's stomach gave an unpleasant lurch. He intended to sit her down and inform her curtly that she kept jeopardizing their precarious working relationship with her unseemly displays of emotion. Things were about to get much worse—she knew it! She could tell just from the look on his face.

Chapter Eight

Jon led the way inside the house, Carole following drearily. I probably deserve the sermon, she thought, but knowing that wouldn't make it go down any easier.

The first inkling she had that he had something else in mind came when he went immediately to the windows and drew the drapes closed. Then, in the blue haze of light that still lingered, Jon walked purposely toward Carole.

"Now we'll finish what we started back at the cabin," he announced.

Carole's heart knocked against her ribs. "What—what do you mean?" she stammered.

"You know what I mean," he said, advancing toward her. A small smile played around his mouth.

He *meant* it—she could see the purpose and intent mingled with desire in his eyes. Her body came singing back to life.

Jon's smile disappeared when his arms went around her. Now his eyes glittered and his face looked taut. "I want you, Carole," he whispered, his lips moving against her hair, her forehead. "God, how I want you! I've ached for days, wanting you!"

Suddenly, in one abrupt motion, he swept her off her feet and into his possessive embrace. With long strides he started toward a dark hallway beyond the living room.

"No," Carole murmured, but it was just a word, utterly without meaning, that glided past her lips. Her heart hammered with its pounding, and the blood rushed hot and swift through her veins.

"Yes," Jon said hoarsely. "I'll have you even if I die for it tomorrow!"

Her head reeled at the almost desperate passion in his voice, and the black hallway spun around her as he charged down it. He reached a door that was almost entirely closed and opened it with a resounding kick.

She was in the master bedroom. Dimly, through the dusky shadows gathered there, Carole saw the expensive yet functional furniture, the earth-tone carpet and matching chair, the big, wide bed.

Jon dropped her on the bed and fell beside her. The bedsprings gave a squeal of protest that sounded like pain. He seized her roughly in his arms, while his lips sought and covered hers.

His lips burned with desire, sending her body into a frenzy of joy, but Carole recognized only passion—not love—in his clutch and burning lips.

Not like this! she longed to cry, but his body pinned her to the bed, and his crushing kiss did not allow her to make a sound.

Fear seized her suddenly. It was irrational fear, for she certainly wasn't a virgin. Jon had once seen to that! But now, nailed to the bed by a desire-gripped man savagely intent on having his way, the drumming of her heart became less passion than genuine terror.

"No!" she broke free long enough to say.

"Yes," Jon muttered in contradiction. Now his lips had found the tender vulnerable curve of her neck, while his hands rose to stroke her breasts.

Though her nipples tightened quite willingly under his touch, fear swelled to enormous proportions in Carole's mind. Jon didn't love her, he just wanted her, and would take her with or without her consent.

"No, Jon, not like this!" she cried, but he appeared deaf to her entreaty.

Like an animal in a trap, Carole began struggling, but her efforts to push away the strong chest and body pressing against hers were brief and futile. Swiftly he caught her small hands in one of his large ones, effectively imprisoning them, while his free hand slipped into the V-neck opening of her shirt.

"Oh, please, Jon—" That was all Carole managed to say before his lips covered hers again. Suddenly her eyes brimmed with tears as hotly burning as his lips. When he felt their spilled wetness Jon drew back. In the near dark of the room Carole saw his annoyed puzzlement change to comprehension.

She lay limp as he peered down at her. With a muffled oath he flung himself away from Carole to lie on the far side of the bed.

Long, agonizing moments crawled past. "Are you really so afraid?" he said, his voice bitter and uneven. "Or is this some act?"

Carole found the edge of a bedsheet and dried her eyes with that. "It's not an act," she said brokenly.

"Pardon me!" he said sarcastically. "From the way you kissed me, I really thought you wanted me, too!"

"I do want you, Jon! Do you think you're the only one who's been aching?" Carole asked, half-laughing, half-sobbing.

"Then why—?" He turned back to her, his eyes blazing with fury and . . . and something else she couldn't read.

"I don't want to be raped, Jon! I want to be loved!" The cry tore from Carole's throat.

When he still stared at her disbelievingly, she whispered, "You used to know how—to perfection!"

"Then show me!" he challenged. "I seem to have forgotten."

She swallowed the lump in her throat, closed her eyes and wound her arms around his strong neck. She drew his dark head back to herself and pressed his unresisting lips with her own. She loved Jon, and in that kiss so freely bestowed Carole tried to show and tell him so. Briefly she traced his perfectly molded lips with her tongue.

His lips parted and she heard his rapid intake of breath. Carole's tongue darted inside his mouth to confront his own. Then his kiss met hers with such stunning sweetness that she felt herself turning to flame. Her body moved, molding itself to him, as their kiss went on and on.

His lips and tongue coaxed hers to respond, trailing tender fire in their wake. Carole realized that her arms were tightening around him, pressing him even closer.

"You taste so good, feel so good, smell so good!" he whispered after a moment. "Your skin—oh, Carole, the feel of your skin—"

When the ardent words ripped from him, interspersed with more kisses, Carole felt the last of her resistance wane. She loved him and wanted him. In all the ways that a man and woman could belong to each other, she wanted to belong to him!

Gently he drew back her shirt, its buttons falling open at his touch. She heard him suck in his breath at the sight of her firm breasts and pink-tipped nipples swelling beneath her lacy bra. His black head fell forward, and his lips pressed over one breast, his breath burning her skin. She trembled beneath his touch, trembling, but without fear. With hands grown impatient, he snatched the single catch at the back of her bra and left her breasts completely free to receive his caresses and moist kisses.

"Jon!" Carole gasped, straining against him as he pulled her shirt and bra away and sent them flying across the room.

He paused long enough to laugh down at her triumphantly. "Now I'm starting to remember."

"Oh, yes—yes, you are," she confessed, pressing his head to her breasts.

While his lips nipped and kissed first one rosy nipple and then its mate, his hands found the buckle of her jeans. He eased the zipper down until it gaped open and his fingertips caressed her flat stomach, dipping daringly lower.

The need to touch him in turn seized Carole irresistibly. Her hand curled around the hairs of his chest, then moved to the restraining buttons of his shirt.

Jon wore no undershirt. As Carole bared his chest, lightly covered with soft curling black hair, she yielded to the impulse to bury her face in its warmth and nuzzle there. Then she raised her head, and their naked chests met to touch and rub together in ecstatic excitement.

His fingers grew even more eager in their downward path. "Oh!" Carole cried as his warm hand curved possessively under the thin nylon panties.

Abruptly he withdrew his hand to rapidly strip away her jeans. Now Carole heard his breath coming in long gasps. "God!" he breathed, surveying, then touching her long sculptured legs. His gaze feasted on the most intimate parts of her, for her thin bikini panties revealed more than they concealed.

His thumbs hooked under their waistband, and a moment later the panties, too, were gone. Carole couldn't feel shame or even shyness, for Jon's sighed "How beautiful you are! So lovely!" held near-reverence.

"It's your turn to undress now, Jon," she said daringly over the thundering beat of her heart.

Quickly he drew away from her. He stood up by the side of the bed and swiftly stripped off his own jeans, shucking his shorts along with them.

Carole gasped with pleasure as she saw him standing nude in the twilight filled room. His olive-skinned body looked exquisite to her. Broad chest, long, flat torso, lean hips, strong legs . . . his physique was even more impressive than she had remembered. She had only a moment to marvel before he moved back beside her on the bed. "You're beautiful, too, Jon," she said in a desire-clogged voice.

Now their unclothed bodies met hungrily, and Carole gloried in the long, hard leanness of him as he covered her and at his eager need. Her mouth fell open beneath the tender onslaught of his, and she grew dizzy from the pleasurable sensations he aroused.

His kisses and caresses resumed, guiding her to a towering pitch of excitement, for he was an utterly uninhibited lover, using his fingertips and tongue and the pressure of his body on hers to give her pleasure. Carole's thighs parted beneath the gentle nudge of his exploring hand and need became an almost savage clamor within her. Eagerly her hands made their own exploration of Jon, and he gasped beneath her touch.

Still he continued to caress her until Carole felt that he was driving her wild. Desire turned to torture as her body cried out for the relief and release that only his could provide. Her hips began to stir erotically, moving on the mattress in an instinctive, age-old rhythm.

"Please, Jon," she whispered against the softness of his lips.

"Yes!" he agreed and decisively lowered his own heated body to hers.

When she felt his swift entry Carole cried out with joy, and the relief of having this act move toward its natural completion.

Gradually the strong strokes of his warm throbbing body moved more deeply within her. Then, when he could go no further, Carole saw the thick eyelashes drop to veil his eyes, and his face became intent as he let the ancient rhythm seize him . . .

. . . and her. Beneath his loving assault on her flesh Carole could only whisper his name, gripped by utter pleasure and delight. She clung to him in growing excitement, meeting his kisses, welcoming each thrust, and their rhythm blended. In perfect rapturous harmony they moved as one being. The rocking-riding motions of love continued on and on, relentlessly, recklessly, deliciously, until passion began splintering Carole's senses.

She felt herself rising as though borne aloft on a wave of pure feeling. She was being lifted higher and higher, striving toward the crest of a great peak. Suddenly she topped it, welded to him, yet free as she had never been before. Then wave and peak and her passionate body were one with his, exploding into a thousand sensations. Radiant colors danced in sunbursts and rainbows before her eyes. At the ultimate moment she heard Jon's cry of ecstasy, felt his body shudder and tremble with his own powerful release and knew he had topped the peak with her.

Slowly, sensuously, they slipped back into reality, one long peaceful moment at a time. Finally Jon's arms loosened, and his mouth covered hers in a long, deep kiss of gratitude. Then, as their bodies reluctantly separated, he lay gasping beside her. Carole turned to curl into the circle of his outflung arm.

When the beat of her maddened, gladdened heart finally began to slow after their crescendo of ecstasy, Carole smiled at Jon and received a languid smile in return. She hoped he wouldn't speak. Right now they were saying everything that needed to be said in this moment of silent communion.

He gave a soft wordless exclamation and dropped his face to rest on her breast, his arms still holding her closely. Long, lazy moments passed. Then, when it was the right time for him to speak, his voice held kindness and just a trace of uncertainty.

"Was it . . . all right for you, Carole?"

"Oh, yes, Jon! Couldn't you tell?" She turned her head and trailed her lips along one crisp black eyebrow. His uncertainty touched her. So he was not quite as self-assured as he seemed.

"I hoped so," he said quietly against her now-soft nipples.

They rested for a long, blissful time, then he raised his head and looked down at her wryly. "You shouldn't be so warm and alluring. You inspire a record in male recovery time! Already I want you again."

His words triggered a deep, sweet tug of desire within Carole. "I was hoping you'd say that," she whispered.

This time his strokes of love were slower, gentler, less driven by urgency, but tenderly passionate in an equally exciting way. Once more they touched the peak of delight together, then dropped down into the warm afterglow.

If I died right at this moment, I wouldn't feel that I'd missed much life has to offer, Carole thought drowsily. Then a sudden practical thought slammed into her head. Carole, if you're not pregnant by now, it will be a minor miracle!

Yet the possibility of motherhood filled her with no fear at all. How I would love to have Jon's child, she thought, aware of a new and entirely different type of hunger.

I'm not even going to worry about it, she decided. I'll just take things one day at a time. It's a modern world now, and I'm certainly old enough to cope.

"What are you thinking about, lovely lady?"

A bedside light clicked on, and Jon peered over at her, his dark eyes as content as she'd ever seen them.

I love you! The words trembled on Carole's lips. Before she could utter them her stomach suddenly rumbled unromantically in the silence. Mortified, Carole blushed. Jon roared with laughter and their magic spell was broken.

"You're starving and no wonder!" he said, rising up on one elbow. "It's all that exercise I've put you through."

She saw the wicked sparkle in his eyes and felt herself blushing. "It's time I fed you," he announced, easing his other arm from beneath her head. "Fortunately I happen to have two big juicy steaks in the refrigerator. Well, get up, Carole," he teased as she continued to lie back, sated and satisfied. "Who do you think will make the salad?"

"Me, I suppose," she sighed, watching as Jon sprang up. He had left their blissful world and moved briskly toward the bathroom. After a moment she heard the shower turned on full blast.

"Come join me!" Jon called.

Carole stretched, yawned, and slipped out of bed. In the bathroom, Jon was a blur behind the glass of the shower stall, steam already rising. She pulled back the sliding door and darted in. His arms came warmly around her waist, hugging her against the hard, soapy length of him.

"Here, wash my back!" he shouted over the drumming of the water and thrust a slippery cake of soap into Carole's hands.

She soaped him thoroughly until Jon's broad back was a thick mass of lather. Then she handed the soap back to him and, with his encouragement, began to knead and scrub his hard, rippling muscles.

"All you're doing is tickling me," he chuckled. He seized the soap again, then swung Carole around. "Let me demonstrate how it's done."

His hands glided strongly and competently over her back, then slipped around to soap her from shoulders to breasts to waist. His slick fingers pressed and kneaded her skin so thoroughly that Carole cried out for mercy.

"I'll show you no mercy!" Jon growled like a movie villain. Beneath the water he swung her back to face him and held her shoulders against the cold tile side of the stall.

"Oh!" Carole screamed. She ducked, managed to elude his grasp, then splashed him.

For several minutes they played and splashed each other in abandon. Then Jon toweled Carole dry and tossed her a long white shirt of his to wear. He pulled on a pair of sports shorts and led the way to the kitchen in his bare feet. By the time Carole had rolled up the sleeves of her floppy shirt, Jon was already sliding two steaks onto the broiler pan.

While the oven preheated and potatoes began to boil in their jackets, Jon helped Carole wash and chop vegetables for a huge salad. "Let's eat outside," he said when the meal was ready, gesturing toward the patio.

At a redwood table there, they sat across from each other, yet close enough that their knees brushed. They attacked their food ravenously, washing it down with long drafts of an excellent Bordeaux.

They ended their meal with coffee. Carole had just taken the last sip of hers when Jon walked around the table, leaned down and took a tendril of her still shower-damp hair, raising it to his lips.

"Darling!" Carole whispered, the word falling naturally from her lips at his loverlike gesture. Swiftly Jon dropped to his knees, and she ran her fingers along his shoulders.

His hands rose to the front of her floppy white shirt, and when he unbuttoned it his fingertips trembled slightly.

For a moment Jon simply gazed at the body that had been given to him so freely, then, his hands sliding beneath the shirt, he wrapped his arms around Carole again.

"I can't keep my hands off you," he breathed. "You looked so young, sitting across from me at dinner. Just like the young girl from Texas I remember. When I came over here I thought I just wanted to hold you. Instead, I want to bury myself in you all over again!"

Abruptly he drew away, rocking back on his heels. "I wouldn't be surprised if I disgust you!"

Irony and self-deprecation mingled again with that touch of uncertainty in Jon's voice.

Carole linked her arms tightly around his neck. "You could never disgust me, Jon."

"Does that mean you actually feel the same?" he said, half-laughing in wonder.

"I might," Carole admitted.

He tipped up her chin, and their lips met while their hands began to move with new certainty on each other's bodies. Gently Jon drew one of Carole's breasts into his mouth, alternately sucking and kissing it until she could feel the fire smoldering deep within her once again. When his hands moved over her so intimately and knowingly, she felt like her bones would melt.

"Just once more," Jon whispered persuasively, and Carole gave an eager yet shy nod.

It was well past midnight when they had finally had enough of each other, and Jon drove Carole home in his Porsche. By then she was so sleepy that she had difficulty staying awake. She was nodding when Jon stopped the car in front of the old two-story house. He turned and dropped a light kiss on Carole's cheek.

"It was perfect, sweetheart," he said, and there seemed to be a little catch in his voice. "I'll call you tomorrow."

She nodded and Jon got out, then crossed to her side and helped her to alight.

Would he really call her the next day? she thought, gripped by sudden fear. Once, after a night much like this, he had left her with the promise to call and she hadn't seen him again for eleven years. I couldn't bear that! Carole thought. I don't think I could live through it again.

She walked beside him, wondering whether to pocket her pride and demand a vow that he would, indeed, remain in touch with her. But she had no claim on him. Despite the hours they'd shared he had not once said he loved her. Then they were on the front porch, where a yellow light gleamed reproachfully over the door.

Carole's courage evaporated in sheer weariness. Automatically her fingers found the right key to unlock the heavy front door. She cherished the light touch of Jon's hand on her shoulder in farewell just before she slipped inside.

Had their lovemaking meant as much to him as it had to her? Carole wondered. Or had he simply wanted her and now, having gotten her, find that enough?

Her brain was too tired to try to puzzle him out. Carole went quickly up the stairs and into her room. There she flung off her clothes, pulled on her pajamas, and tumbled into bed. Sleep claimed her almost instantly. The fresh air, the long walk and—most of all—their abandoned ecstasies had left her exhausted.

Just as she tumbled headlong into a dark, welcoming well of sleep Carole heard a faint tap at her door. "Carole, are you in there?" a soft young voice whispered. "Carole?"

But she was too deeply asleep to stir, much less reply.

Carole sat at the desk in her small office at the library, bending a paperclip back and forth between her restless fingers. In front of her, in the typewriter, was a blank sheet of paper, the same sheet that had been there for three long days.

Three days! Once again Carole felt the heaviness of her frustrated heart. Anxiety and anger, fear and the gnawing, galling feeling of having known all of this before gripped her throat in a vise.

Three days without a word from Jon. It was like history repeating itself. By now she had run out of alibis and excuses for him. Yet still she started up hopefully any time she heard footsteps in the hallway outside.

Between her fingers the paperclip snapped into two useless pieces. Carole turned to fling them into the wastebasket where quite a number of similar casualties resided, and the blank paper in the typewriter mocked her again. For the first time that she could ever remember, she was too distraught to work.

If Jon should walk in right now, she would tell him to drop dead, Carole thought heatedly. But the prickle of tears behind her eyelids told quite a different story. If he walks in right now, I'll probably throw my arms around him and make an even bigger fool of myself than I have before, she realized dismally.

If only she didn't love him so much! If only she

didn't want him so badly! The hunger within her that he'd assuaged so skillfully with lips and tongue, with the touch of his body on hers, within hers, clamored anew. *How* could he simply walk away from hours like those they'd shared?

She didn't know. She would never understand. She hadn't understood once before, either. All she knew was that Jon had the power to excite her, thrill her and make her heart brim over with love as no other man ever had.

Her ears pricked up again at the sound of footsteps, but these passed disappointingly by, as most had. Twice, though, in those last agonizing days her door had opened to admit visitors.

The first time it was Tom Kaufman. Carole had practically forgotten all about Dr. Kaufman in the last few weeks of blinding happiness spent with Jon. Guiltily she lurched out of her chair to welcome him.

Tom looked well and fit, a casual figure in a string-knit shirt of summer blue that matched the blue of his eyes and darker blue pants. To Carole's surprise, he apologized to *her*. He had not meant to neglect her or their project, he explained, but he had been quite busy at the college.

They reviewed Carole's tapes and notes, all that she and Jon had accomplished together, and Carole could see that the professor was pleased. "Why, this is going marvelously," he enthused an hour later. "I think a really fine book is going to be the result, one that you and Jon can take pride in."

"Thank you," Carole said even more guiltily, for she had certainly done nothing that day to justify his praise, although earlier she had indeed worked conscientiously for long, hard hours.

"Lois tells me how busy you and Jon have been, running hither, thither and yon," Tom went on, setting down a stack of Carole's neatly typed pages.

Lois! Carole had almost forgotten about the attractive young widow, too. Now her heart burned with jealousy. So Jon had been seeing and talking to Lois all during the time he'd worked with her! She didn't know why the thought made her so angry or why, at the same time, she was filled with such utter desolation.

"I didn't know Lois was so well advised as to the state of our work," Carole said stiffly to Tom.

His eyes ran shrewdly over her face, not missing her state of agitation. "You look like you just bit into a very sour apple," he observed. "I can only surmise that you are smitten all over again by the very handsome and sought-after Jon Haughton."

"Is it that obvious, Tom?" Carole cried in dismay.

"To me it is. But, remember, you told me of your past history with the gentleman, and I've had the opportunity to observe the two of you together on several occasions." Tom stopped for a breath. "While it isn't my place to say this, I'm going to anyway: I don't think you have a thing to fear from Lois. She and Jon are good friends, nothing more."

"You don't know that for sure," Carole said, still agonized.

"Oh, but I think I do." He gave her a small, diffident smile. "You see, I myself have spent quite a number of evenings with Lois and her youngsters."

"You have?" Carole's eyes flew open wide.

"Yes. That's one reason why I feel a trifle guilty toward you, my dear. Because I've been over here in Green Grove on several evenings without your ever knowing it. Oh, I always *intended* to call, but Lois and I would start talking and I'd lose track of time. That's why I know her recent contacts with Jon have been in brief phone calls."

"You and Lois . . . oh, Tom, that's wonderful!" Carole cried as relief sang sweetly through her veins.

He held up a warning hand. "Hey, don't get that matchmaking look on your face. Lois and I are just starting to get acquainted, though I like and respect her more all the time. She's been quite a help to me. Why, that woman seems to positively enjoy poring over dusty court records. She's unearthed several documents concerning the Coldrens and Haughtons that I doubt I would have found otherwise."

"Tell her that I'm grateful, too," Carole said, sinking back in her chair.

"Don't get too comfortable there," Tom smiled, "because I intend to take you to lunch."

Willingly Carole reached for her purse, and they went off together to the neighborhood cafe.

Tom's visit had been a welcome, relief-inspiring diversion during the empty days. But her cousin Susan's visit proved more disturbing.

"Am I interrupting a busy author at work?" Susan had asked that morning, poking her plain and bony little face around the door of Carole's office.

"Not at all. Come in," Carole urged with more warmth than she actually felt. That instinctive wariness toward Susan tightened her muscles once again. It was really too bad that the frail woman now affected her that way, for Susan had been her faithful pen pal for years. Of course, Susan had also been the one who ran to Uncle Buck Coldren, and while Carole had forgiven her for that, she would never trust her again.

"Tell me," she said rapidly, "did you get the travelers off to Arizona?"

"Oh, yes. Blake and Yvonne left this morning," Susan said, taking the chair across from Carole's desk.

Carole had heard, of course, of their decision to leave Green Grove. Blake had been unable to find work here, and the couple hoped that Arizona's warm, dry climate would improve his arthritis. "Did Wynne go along, too?" Carole asked curiously.

"Yes. She's closed her apartment and put her

furniture in storage." Susan gave a little sigh.
"Wynne's been bored this last year. She says
she's just going along to help Yvonne with the
driving, but, frankly, I don't think she'll be
back. It's strange to think of Green Grove without Blake and Wynne. They've always been a
part of our life here."

"Yes," Carole said briskly. "I hope they'll all
be happy. That desert country is beautiful. I
spent a vacation at a dude ranch in Arizona
once."

"You've done a lot of interesting things,"
Susan said a trifle wistfully. "You and Jon both."

"I suppose." Carole purposely kept her reply
brief. She didn't want a discussion of Jon, not
now of all times.

"All I ever wanted was just to marry Reggie
and have babies," Susan blurted, "but only half
my dream has come true."

A discussion of babies was also not very reassuring for Carole at this particular time, yet she
made herself look at Susan encouragingly.
"You're still young. Maybe you will yet, Susan."

"I don't think so." Susan's thin face began to
crumble.

"Susan, what is it?" Carole said in alarm.

Susan fumbled in her handbag for a tissue. "I
saw a doctor in Asheville yesterday. A specialist."

Carole felt the blood drain from her face.
"Susan, what—?" She stopped, unable to say
another word.

"Oh, don't look like that, Carole! I'm not sick

like poor Blake. I saw Dr. Wysinger because he's a specialist in infertility."

"Oh," Carole said softly.

"Reggie wants children as much as I do. We just rattle around in that house we built for a big family!"

"Susan, what did the doctor say?" Carole asked.

"He made all the usual tests, but I know what the results will be. Reggie and I have had them before and we always check out fine. But Dr. Wysinger threw a new wrinkle at me. He said lots of women don't get pregnant if their body weight is down even as much as ten pounds. He said if I'd relax, eat more and gain weight . . . But, Carole, I can't! I stay tense and nervous, and food just sticks in my throat."

"Susan." Compassionately Carole reached across to pat the small hands opposite hers. "Is anything else bothering you? Is Reggie—?"

"No! He's the best husband in the world," Susan said aggressively.

Carole nodded, although she knew in her heart that Susan's protests didn't ring true. *Something* was eating at her cousin—something so serious that it prevented Susan from eating properly. But Carole was also wise enough to know that she couldn't force an unwilling confidence. Instead, while Susan struggled to control her emotions, Carole went to the nearby soda machine and came back with drinks for them. It was all she had been able to think of . . .

Now another set of footsteps came down the

hall, jarring Carole from her lethargy. Once again she sat up eagerly, hopefully, until she realized that the light, rather hesitant steps could not be Jon's.

The door opened slowly and Carole blinked in surprise at sight of the handsome woman standing there. She was in her forties, tall and slender, with marvelous grave dark eyes and short hair that was naturally silvered. The few lines on her face were those of character.

Although Carole had never met her, she recognized the woman even before she spoke. "Miss Coldren, I'm Sally Haughton Rodgers."

"Of course you are," Carole said, rising automatically from her chair. Jon would look very much like this woman in a few more years.

"I'm Jon's older sister. Terry Rodgers's mother," the woman went on, explaining unnecessarily.

"Yes. I'm so glad to meet you!" Carole exclaimed warmly.

She saw Sally Rodgers draw back almost visibly from her enthusiastic response. Only then did Carole note the chill in the older woman's eyes, and she felt a similar chill drop over her.

"My brother had to leave town unexpectedly," Mrs. Rodgers went on, her voice stiff. "He asked me to deliver a note to you." She reached into the pocket of her denim wrap-around skirt and drew the paper out slowly, handing it over to Carole.

Carole seized the note, tearing it open with

fingers that shook from eagerness. Perhaps it was rude to grab it and read it in front of Mrs. Rodgers, but she had to know what Jon had written to her. She had to!

Carole, I've been called to Raleigh for a few days' consultation on the dam. I'll see you as soon as I get back. Don't work too hard.

Jon

The note certainly didn't say the words Carole's heart longed most to hear. Still, she could have kissed the black-scrawled message. Slowly she raised her eyes to Sally Rodgers, not knowing what was written on her face but feeling as though a light had been turned on inside her.

At least this time Jon had cared enough to write her a note!

She saw Sally staring at her curiously, as though disbelieving the radiance in Carole's face. The woman's own handsome features hardened. "Please don't hurt my brother," she said tersely. "Jon's been hurt enough!"

Dumbfounded, Carole stared at Sally, then she understood. The older woman was referring to Jon's fiancée who had died.

Before she could muster a reply, Sally spoke again, and this time Carole heard despair in the woman's voice. "Mixing Coldrens and Haughtons always hurts someone. Oh, please, leave my family alone!" She turned as though to go, then swung back for a parting shot. "Tell your little cousin the same thing. Tell her to leave my family alone!"

With that, Sally Rodgers departed, moving with Jon's lithe, swift gait. Carole stared after her, haunted by the woman's last words. "Your little cousin," she'd said. Whom had she meant?

Betsy, of course.

Chapter Nine

*A*nother long day had inched painfully past. Time had a curious quality, Carole reflected when she lay in bed on Friday night. When she was with Jon, the hours fairly flew. When she was without him, they passed on feet of lead.

Was he really coming back to her, as his note had said? And, if he did, would she ever, ever again hear him utter those words that once he'd said so freely, "I love you, Carole"?

I'm dying of longing for him, she thought, pressing the aching length of her body against the crisp bottom sheet. How she wished he lay here with her now!

Stop it, she told herself tiredly. Dwelling on memories did no good and only frustrated her further. It was already quite late, Carole knew. She needed to sleep so she'd be rested enough to work well the next day and make up for her days of agonizing idleness.

Think of something else, she commanded herself.

There was Betsy to think about. Although Carole had sought out the girl that evening and tried to encourage her confidence, Betsy's mouth had taken on a stubborn set.

"I thought I heard you call to me the other night," Carole said to her quietly. "I'm sorry I was so close to sleep I couldn't answer."

"I didn't call you," Betsy said, but her bright eyes flickered away uneasily from Carole's.

Carole tried a sterner tack. "Betsy, if you've been seeing Terry Rodgers, I need to know about it. Now!"

The girl's eyes looked startled, but her mouth only tightened. "I haven't seen Terry except at school," she said defiantly. "Now that school is over for the summer, I won't be seeing him at all."

"Betsy, there are rumors of trouble between the Coldrens and Haughtons. I need to know the truth before something awful happens again," Carole insisted.

"I don't know anything about any trouble," Betsy denied. "I've told you that before."

Carole struck with her strongest ammunition. "I talked to Terry's mother today. Mrs. Rodgers seems to think you and Terry are involved somehow."

"Well, we're not!" Betsy blazed, yet a wayward muscle leaped beneath her smooth jaw, and Carole realized that the girl felt pulled in two directions. Had Terry, or someone else, extracted a promise of silence from her? Although Carole suspected that, in light of Betsy's constant denials she had no recourse but to give up in defeat.

At least reviewing the scene with the difficult girl drew Carole nearer to sleep. She yawned, feeling her grip on reality beginning to loosen, and she slid down deeper into the bed.

Several hours later Carole awoke as abruptly as though someone had bent down and shaken her shoulder. Tense and alert, she peered into the velvet darkness. The lighted dial on her bedside clock read 3:30.

Why had she awakened? Carole wondered. Of course there were sounds galore in the old house. It creaked, settling down on its foundations. Through Carole's open window came the squeaking of the porch swing. Yet some sound far more alien than those had awakened her, and Carole tried to reach back through the veil of sleep to remember what it was. Stealthy footsteps going back and forth in front of her door, was that it? If so, they were gone now.

Memories gripped Carole, intermingling with the events of the previous day. Her mind flew again to that terse note that Sally Rodgers had delivered. Why hadn't she just torn it up? Carole puzzled. She obviously didn't approve of Jon's having anything to do with her. But remembering those character lines on the woman's fine-featured face, Carole felt grudging admiration. Sally would not destroy a note, however much she might disapprove of its intended recipient. To do so would have been dishonorable, and plainly Jon's sister was a woman of honor.

Why didn't Jon ever answer my long-ago letter? Carole thought suddenly, stirred by surprise. It was completely out of character for him not to have done so.

Carole still remembered every extravagant word she'd written him. Now excerpts from that letter leaped into her mnd: "I want you so badly and I love you so much! I know it's just been a week, but it seems like you're never coming back from that bridge! Oh, Jon, you were right that we shouldn't be slipping around. As soon as you're back I want you to come to the front door for me. I'll be so proud to introduce you to Uncle Paul and Aunt Louise. Maybe when I go back to Texas you can come and meet my mother, too. Oh, please call me when you get back. Please call me the *minute* you come back!"

Carole would not write such a letter now. Both her professional training and the wisdom of maturity left her too cautious for such forthrightness. But the eager seventeen-year-old she'd once been had known no such inhibitions.

Now she blinked into the darkness, still puzzled that Jon, a man of honor, had ignored her letter. Then she became aware of several other sounds and noises. Someone was up and stirring at this beastly hour. It must be Betsy, since she was the only other person who slept upstairs.

An almost-forgotten memory nudged her. Once, during that summer eleven years ago, Carole had been awakened by similar strange night noises. Then she had leaped out of bed eagerly and darted to the window. Jon had already been two weeks late in returning to her, but Carole had not yet abandoned all hope. On that particular occasion the noises had come from the street below. Peering around the curtain, Carole had seen the revolving blue light on the top of a sheriff's car parked near the great spruce tree.

Uncle Buck had apprehended a would-be burglar on that night, Carole recalled.

Good heavens! Startled, she sat bolt upright in bed. Had someone broken into the house? Was that the explanation for all the strange sounds she continued to hear?

Carole's heartbeat accelerated as she slipped from bed. Out of habit she groped for her slippers, then decided against wearing them, remembering their loose soles and the slapping sound they made on hardwood floors. Better to stay barefoot if she intended to investigate.

Carole slipped noiselessly through her door and out into the dark hall, just in time to see Betsy dart out of her own bedroom.

The girl was dressed in jeans and a pullover sweater, a jacket slung around her shoulders. In one hand she carried her purse by its long shoulder strap. In her other hand was a small suitcase.

For a moment Carole stood paralyzed, watching while the girl tiptoed down the stairs. Then, coming out of shock, she moved into action.

"Betsy!" Carole hissed.

Betsy stopped, threw a furtive look over her shoulder and saw Carole standing there at the top of the stairs.

"Where do you think you're going at this hour?" Carole demanded.

"I'm going with Terry. We're going to get married, and you can't stop us! We love each other. Tell Mama and Daddy that I'll . . . I'll write them later!"

"Betsy!" Carole cried, but the girl had already fled through the downstairs hallway and plunged out into the night.

Her heart banging against her ribs, Carole started after her. She stopped when she reached the landing. Outside she could hear a truck's motor spring to life, and the futility of dashing barefoot and in her skimpy pajamas after an eloping cousin was borne in on her.

For a moment Carole stood rigid. What could she do to stop those crazy, impulsive kids before they made a serious mistake? What could she possibly do?

Carole didn't know—but if Jon were home, *he* would know. Perhaps he had returned by now! Carole flew back up the stairs, rushing for the upstairs phone. Please let him be home! she prayed. His note had said that he'd only be away a few days. Since it was the weekend now, surely he would be back.

Hastily she flipped through the phone book to obtain his number, then she dialed it rapidly. Her heart began to sink anew when, after three rings, there had been no answer.

Just as Carole was about to give up and replace the receiver in its cradle she heard a click. "Hello?" said Jon, sleepy-voiced.

"Jon, it's Carole," she said shakily. Oh, how wonderful he sounded!

"Carole! What's wrong?" Instantly he was awake and alert.

Quickly she explained. Before she had finished, Jon swore under his breath. "Those fools! Those crazy young damn fools! Terry is seventeen. How could he possibly support a wife?"

"Betsy is only sixteen," Carole whispered, then waited, trembling.

Jon was silent for a moment, and Carole could almost hear him thinking. "I'll be over as quickly as I can," he said at last. "Get dressed. Write your aunt and uncle a note. Tell them what's happened, but urge them not to panic. Tell them we're going after those harebrained kids. Then, if you have time, fix us a thermos of coffee. Got that?"

"I've got it," Carole said shakily.

"O.K.," he said, and hung up abruptly.

Carole found herself clutching the silent phone while she repeated the same words over and over. "Thank God, thank God. . . ."

Carole was sitting on the front porch steps, waiting for Jon, when his headlights swept around the corner. She ran to the Bronco as Jon, without alighting, threw the door open for her. She leaped inside and they were off.

"I brought the coffee," she said, hugging the warm thermos. "I also helped myself to a package of cinnamon rolls out of Aunt Louise's freezer. They'll thaw fast."

"Good," Jon said, his voice clipped.

Carole darted a glance at him. His face, seen in the frail dashboard light, looked grim and angry. He was furious with his nephew, she realized. Nevertheless, she wished he would show her some signs of personal awareness.

"How have you been?" she asked him almost shyly. After all, it had been almost a week since they'd seen each other.

"I've been all right," he said as brusquely as before.

Chilled and hurt by Jon's reaction, Carole huddled in her seat. I know he's tired and mad and probably not very communicative anyway when he's been woken in the middle of the night, but at least he could say a civil word to me! Resentment and hurt rose like twin demons inside her.

"I'm sorry, Carole." Almost as if Jon could read her troubled, unhappy thoughts, he chose the right time to speak. Far more reassuring was the light pressure of his hand. It dropped onto her shoulder, finding, as if by magic, the juncture where her jacket opened over her knit shirt. His hand rested on her shirt, just over the skin of her collarbone.

Tears of relief stung Carole's eyes even as her body quickened in response to his light touch. I love him so much, I'm grateful for any crumb he tosses me, she thought in amazement.

"I'd like to kill that young devil," Jon muttered, and she knew his thoughts were still on Terry.

"I'd rather like to get my hands around Betsy's neck, too," she admitted and he gave a short laugh.

"Jon, can they really get married?" Carole asked after a moment.

Now his hand moved upward, sliding beneath the hair that flowed over her shoulders. "They might manage it," he groaned. "I stopped long enough to check on marriage requirements in my almanac. They can both pass for eighteen, I'm afraid, and there's no waiting period either in North Carolina or Tennessee. If they go into Tennessee their chances might be better. Only a blood test is required there."

"Is that where we're headed, then, Tennessee?" she asked.

"Ultimately, if they're not where I think they'll be on this side of the state line."

"Where is that?" Carole inquired.

"The town of Cherokee. You once met our Indian friend, Willie Running-Brook. He lives just this side of the Great Smoky Mountains National Park. He taught Terry and me and most of the other Haughtons how to hunt and track game in the wilderness. Terry's always gone running off to see Willie when he's in trouble. I have a hunch he's done it this time, too. Also, he may have some idea that Willie could arrange a tribal marriage."

"Would he?" asked Carole apprehensively.

"I hope not," came the dry reply as his hand slid gently down to the nape of her neck. "Willie's always shown a lot of common sense."

Jon fell silent again, and Carole no longer pressed him to talk. She looked through the windshield at the dark, broken only by frosty patches of fog. When her ears popped she knew they were climbing high up into the mountains. Yellow highway signs warned of curves ahead, and the road began to snake.

It was chilly and dark, and Carole felt miserably tired. But she was with Jon, so that made both the eerie night and her physical discomfort trifling matters. Impulsively she reached up to cover Jon's hand and felt his fingers link through hers.

"You feel good," he muttered, adding, "I missed you, you know."

"I missed you, too!"

Then the curves in the road became serpentine twists, and Jon needed both his hands for the steering wheel. Carole sat beside him, trying to stay awake and not yawn while her mind played and replayed his casual words: "I missed you, you know."

Just before dawn they stopped at a mountain overlook where they drank the last of the coffee and ate a couple of soggy sweet rolls.

In the cool grayish light the mighty mountains were crowned with haze, then the rim of the tallest peak turned gold against the whitening sky and suddenly the bright yellow sun peeped over. The rims of nearby mountains began to glow and pinken.

"Let's get out and stretch our legs," Jon suggested, and Carole followed him willingly. They walked to the overlook rail and watched the panorama around them. From the thick trees nearby came the jubilant morning songs of birds as they preened, chirped and celebrated the dawn.

Great puffs of haze rose steaming, like white smoke on the mountains, and Carole turned to Jon questioningly. "You're viewing the Great Smoky Mountains," he said, answering her up-lifted eyebrow.

"Marvelous," she breathed, watching as the "smoke" lifted in puffy balls and floated upward toward the pale sky.

When the sun rose higher Carole could see that the vast timbered green mountains plunged down to form deep gorges. Far below lay smooth, heavily grassed meadows. Looking miles down, she saw a glistening ribbon of river.

"We'd better be on our way," Jon said, and, regretfully, Carole turned away from the splendor before her.

She had hoped he might touch her again or kiss her, but Jon made no move in her direction. Rather, he seemed determined to continue their journey as quickly as possible.

Carole got back into her seat, aware of a wisp of headache throbbing at her temples, mute evidence of her profound weariness. When they were moving down the highway again she closed her eyes, intending just to rest them for a moment. Instead she was almost immediately asleep.

The sun was higher and hotter when she

awoke, and she discovered that her head had slipped quite naturally onto Jon's shoulder. The hard pillow had felt so natural and right that Carole seemed to have slept away most of her fatigue. She felt rested and hopeful, very hopeful. After all, she was with *him*.

She blinked, still not stirring, but raised her eyes enough to survey Jon, drinking in the sight of the strong, clean lines of his face. The straight, proud nose, the firm chin, the faint hollows at his temples and below his cheekbones, the long line of his throat. Unconsciously Carole moistened her lips, her body quickening with renewed hungry desire.

Despite the attraction he held for her, Jon looked something less than his usual immaculate self. The bright morning light revealed a dark shadow of beard on his cheeks. His thick black hair was rumpled. He would probably look like this when he awoke each morning. Carole gazed at the few silvered hairs at his temples. Oh, what a beautiful, distinguished older man Jon would be in fifteen or twenty years!

Determinedly she looked away from the tantalizing sight of him and gazed out at her surroundings. Most of the haze had faded from the mountain tops, though occasional smoky wisps still rose.

They were on a twisting, winding mountain road where it was impossible to drive very fast. Giant, green trees overshadowed the highway, wearing the light, bright green leafage of spring. Stately pines interspersed among them were a darker olive green. Jagged rocks, covered with lichen and moss, abounded, wood ferns jutting out of their crevices.

What fabulous country this is, Carole thought, admiring the blooming dogwood and the occasional patches of yellow wildflowers. A tangle of honeysuckle attracted her attention, and yellow butterflies rose in a cloud to dance by the window beside their vehicle.

I want to stay here in North Carolina for the rest of my life, Carole thought, balling her hands into fists, so intense was her longing. I want to stay here with Jon and see him rumpled and bearded and, yes, even grumpy in the morning. I want to——

"So you finally decided to wake up." He looked down at her, smiling faintly, before turning his attention back to the road.

"Where are we?" Carole asked, stretching her cramped legs.

"Almost there," he said reassuringly. "We've just passed through the town of Cherokee, and we're close to Willie's place now. We're on the Indian reservation."

"Until I met Willie I hadn't realized there were Indians in North Carolina," Carole mused.

"Yes. The Cherokees hunted these mountains long before the white man ever arrived. They're the ones who named the mountains 'The Great Smokies.' Unfortunately for most of the Cherokees, they were later herded up and marched off to Oklahoma. Willie is a descendant of the few Indians who managed to escape capture by hiding in the woods."

"If I'd been an Indian I would have hidden in these deep woods, too," Carole said fiercely.

Jon threw her another swift look. "So would I," he agreed. "At least I'd have tried. Hey, we're here!" They were rapidly approaching a small frame house set at the foot of a vast mountain. Carole heard Jon's chuckle of satisfaction, and he jerked a thumb toward a white and red pickup truck that carried the Haughtons' familiar insignia. "And look who else is here—our kids!"

"Oh, Jon, you were right!" In her excitement and relief Carole squeezed the strong arm next to her.

Did he deliberately move it away from her eager fingers or was the gesture necessary for him to wheel into the clearing and stop behind the truck? Carole tried to think it was the latter.

The door to the house stood open. Behind the simple structure she could see a barn, a wooden privy, split-rail fences that enclosed a garden and a pen for animals. There were also a large number of beehives.

A short, copper-colored man working in the garden straightened up at their approach. He wore faded jeans and a T-shirt that had been washed so many times that its original color was impossible to detect.

"There's Willie," Jon said with relief, switching off the engine.

"He looks just the same," Carole observed.

"Come on," Jon called to her as he leaped out and moved with his quick graceful strides to clasp the hands of the Cherokee, who also hurried to meet him.

"Glad you've come," Willie was saying matter-of-factly to Jon when Carole joined them. "Good to see you again, Miss Coldren. I wondered what I was gonna do with that wild-eyed boy and the pretty little thing he fetched up here. They tell me they want to get married."

"We know," Jon nodded.

"I told 'em it wasn't very likely they could manage that on a Saturday. All the state offices are closed," Willie continued.

Carole and Jon's eyes locked with chagrin, then Jon burst out laughing. "Willie, you're wonderful!" he said, clapping his much shorter friend on the shoulder. "Neither Carole nor I had realized that they couldn't get married on a weekend."

"Where are they?" Carole asked softly, enjoying the sight of Jon's unabashed merriment.

Willie pointed toward a path that led back behind his house. "Walked down to the waterfall. Guess they didn't know what to do next. I was about to go fetch 'em. My wife's started cooking breakfast."

"We'll get them," Jon offered. His hand brushed Carole's shoulder quite impersonally, and he guided her toward the path.

It led up and around rocks and threaded through massive stands of trees. They could hear a trilling creek long before they saw it splashing merrily on its way downhill. Dandelions gone to fuzz and river fern grew along the path. So did wild azaleas in bright colors of melon and peach.

They rounded a bend in the path and stopped. High above them sparkling water cascaded down, creating a gentle roar. Standing before them, at the foot of the foaming, plunging stream, were Betsy and Terry. They had their backs to the older couple, their arms around each other's waists.

While they watched, Terry lowered his head to Betsy's, and the girl went up on tiptoes to meet his gentle kiss. Tears smarted in Carole's eyes. Once she and Jon must have looked just as this young couple did now—troubled and idealistic and achingly in love.

Carole felt Jon's gaze on her and knew he had seen her tears. He cleared his throat as though something constricted it. "I've just had an idea," he said, his voice low and huskier than usual. "Instead of us tackling them like gangbusters, I'll talk to Betsy. You take Terry."

Terry Rodgers, nearly six feet tall and almost eighteen, obviously knew that grown men don't cry. So he clenched his fists and bit his lip while he walked beside Carole along the banks of the stream. The story poured out of him in fits and starts. With a black eye and a purple bruise on his chin, he looked very vulnerable to Carole.

"I always knew Betsy liked me, see, but I

didn't even dare to phone her. The one time I ever mentioned her to my mom she had a fit! Mom made it plain that I wasn't *ever* to call or date Betsy.

"Maybe I wouldn't have, either . . . except that I met you, Carole, and you seemed so friendly and nice, too. So I took a chance and called Betsy. She was so darn glad to hear from me. . . .

"All we wanted"—his eyes brightened suspiciously once again—"was just to *see* each other. Have regular dates. Go to games and parties together. But Betsy knew her folks would carry on just like mine. We really didn't want to sneak around, but what could we do? When school let out we couldn't even see each other!"

"I understand, Terry," Carole said soothingly.

"Do you? Anyway, day before yesterday, Betsy and I were sitting in my truck when my cousin Lon stormed over. He'd warned me once to keep away from Betsy, and when he saw us there he pulled me out of the truck and hit me. I tried to defend myself, but Lon's strong and he's mean. He knocked me down again, in front of Betsy!"

Clearly the humiliation of that moment still burned in the young man's soul. "Lon told me to keep my distance from 'any Coldren wench.' *That's* what he called Betsy, and he said the licks he'd already landed weren't anything compared to what I'd get if he ever saw me with her again.

"We didn't know what to do, Carole! Betsy wanted to talk to you about it—she was really scared—but I guess I changed her mind. So we started talking about running away and getting married. That way the Coldrens and Haughtons would have to let us be together!"

"But, Terry, have you really thought about what marriage entails?" Carole asked sensibly. "A married couple can't live on movie and gas money. You have to pay rent and buy groceries and a hundred other things!"

"I can get a job," Terry replied. "I know lots about cars."

"But would you want to do that for the rest of your life?" she persisted. "Pumping gas and towing stalled cars? I thought you wanted to go to college and become an engineer like Jon—"

"I did want that," he cut in, "but I don't want to give up Betsy!"

"I don't know why you should have to," Carole said, after a moment's reflection. "I'll help you and Betsy all I can in dealing with your families. Jon will, too, I'm sure."

"You'd really do that?" he said hopefully.

"I sure will." Carole reached for his large, work-calloused hand and squeezed it. "First, though, you've got to go back and face the music."

"Starting with Uncle Jon!" he groaned.

"He was young once himself, Terry. I think he'll understand." Carole spoke with more assurance than she actually felt. Please let it be true, she thought, as she led the way back up the path where Jon and Betsy stood waiting.

Willie was waiting for them, too. "If you folks

don't come on in the house and eat, you're gonna see one mad Indian woman," he warned.

"I'm ready," Betsy said breathlessly. "In fact, I'm starved!" Her eyes met Carole's warily, in much the same way that Terry was regarding his fearsome uncle Jon.

"I'm hungry, too," Terry echoed.

Betsy threw a grateful look at Jon, then she reached for Terry's hand and the two of them bounded back in the direction of Willie's small house. Already they were children again.

Carole and Jon followed at a more sedate pace. "They don't actually want to get married," Carole informed him. "They just want the opportunity to date each other and permission to be in love. At least, that's the way Terry feels."

"Betsy, too, thank God," he said feelingly. "I questioned her pretty closely, and apparently they haven't gone beyond the kissing and hand-holding stage."

"That's good." Carole felt color rising in her cheeks. "I didn't even think to ask Terry about that. But I did tell him I'd try to help them with their folks. Will you?"

Jon nodded emphatically. "It's far better to know where the kids are going and when they'll be home than to try to keep them from seeing each other. That's not going to work with them . . . any more than it once did with us. They've already proved it." Jon stopped, his face reflective. "Betsy did say one thing that was rather sweet and silly and noble. She said, 'Mr. Haughton, the only way to ever stop this awful feud and make the two families friends is to make them kin.' She seemed to think that if she and Terry married, it would help end all the years of enmity."

Carole's heart gave a leap in her breast. "I once thought the same thing myself."

"Did you?" Jon shot her a strange, unfathomable look.

They fell into step again, Jon's shoulder touching Carole's, but only in the most cursory way. Together they went up to the house and inside, where Willie's wife waited with a huge breakfast of sugar-cured ham, scrambled eggs and stacks of fluffy corncakes served with honey from Willie's own hives.

Chapter Ten

An hour later the four bid farewell to their Indian friends and returned to their vehicles. "If I let you and Betsy ride together, can I trust you to head back home?" Jon asked his nephew dryly.

Terry nodded. "Thanks, Uncle Jon!" he said fervently.

Jon clapped his nephew's shoulder affectionately. "Carole and I will stop in Cherokee to phone ahead to the families. Let's plan to meet in about three hours at the Hillside Cafe. I'll treat you kids to lunch."

"Lunch! How can you even think about food after that breakfast we just ate?" Carole asked when she and Jon settled again into the Bronco.

"I can't," he agreed readily. "But teenagers have voracious appetites, in case you've forgotten."

At a pay phone by the main highway, Carole phoned the Coldrens; then it was Jon's turn to call the Haughtons with the welcome news that the kids had been found and were on their way back home.

"I warned Sally not to be too tough on Terry," Jon said as they drove off again. "In fact, I suggested that she and Dick, her husband, go over and introduce themselves to Betsy's parents. Surely four civilized adults who love their kids ought to be able to work things out reasonably."

"That's remarkable." Carole flashed him a startled glance. "Why, it's almost exactly what I told Uncle Paul and Aunt Louise."

"Maybe we're reading each other's minds," Jon said wryly.

No, they weren't, Carole thought while the Bronco gathered speed again, and silence dropped between them. If Jon could read her mind, he'd know how much she wanted him to touch her, hold her, even clasp her on the shoulder as he'd done to Willie and Terry.

I'm burning up with wanting him, she thought bleakly, seeing the faint tremor in her fingers as they lay loosely in her lap. Either Jon doesn't know or he just doesn't care! She hungered to feel his mouth on hers, his hands cupping her breasts, the whole long, sinewy length of him pressed against her. Carole sat alone with her silent yearnings, her body quivering faintly beneath her clothes.

If only he'd stop, Carole reflected, I'd beg him to take me here, in the grass by the side of the road. Perhaps it's just as well Jon *can't* read my thoughts. We'd probably be arrested!

Jon stopped only once and then at their prearranged destination. There he drank a cup of coffee while Carole sipped iced tea, but, as he'd predicted, Betsy and Terry wolfed down hamburgers and french fries.

"How much farther do we have to go?" Carole asked when they were moving down the highway again, following Terry's truck.

"Another hour." Jon paused to rub a hand over his face, and Carole was suddenly aware of his fatigue.

"You're tired, Jon," she said solicitously.

"Yeah. That's the difference between being eighteen and thirty-five. When Terry and I were in the men's room back at the restaurant I asked him if he felt awake enough to keep driving. He said he felt swell. I'm afraid I can't say the same. I spent a very hectic week in Raleigh, and I'd barely gotten to sleep last night when you called."

"Would you like me to drive the rest of the way?" Carole offered.

He threw her a look of sheer gratitude. "You wouldn't mind?"

I wouldn't mind doing anything to help you! she thought passionately. Aloud she merely said, "I don't mind at all."

Jon pulled over and they changed places. Immediately he leaned back in the seat Carole had vacated and closed his eyes, though when she ground the gears pulling out, he cracked open one lid to look at her dubiously. When Carole shifted the other gears more skillfully Jon gave a little sigh, and a moment later his even breathing assured Carole that he was fast asleep.

She drove automatically, following the white truck and trying not to think of the exhausted man sleeping beside her. But Carole couldn't resist stealing an occasional look at him. Jon's face was softened, the sculptured mouth parted slightly. He looked almost as vulnerable as Terry had. Tenderness swelled in Carole's heart, sharing space with the desire that still seethed there.

At last she saw the Green Grove city limits sign. Terry's truck slowed in obedience to the speed laws, so Carole slowed, too. The change in motion awoke Jon. He sat up, rubbing the sleep from his eyes.

"Pull over," he directed her quietly. "I can take it from here."

Jon chose the shortest, most direct route to Poplar Street and nodded with satisfaction when he saw the white truck stopped before Betsy's house. He braked by the blue spruce tree, but made no movement to get out.

Surprised, Carole turned to look at him. "I see Sally's car in the driveway," he remarked conversationally, then he turned to her. "Let's skip the family remonstrances. We've found the kids and brought them back. Let their parents take over now."

Carole felt her mouth opening to form a silent "Oh?"

"Do you want to come home with me?" Jon said to her abruptly.

Every nerve in Carole's body soared in exhilaration. She could feel the blood beginning to

214

race through her veins, yet something about his almost curt inquiry rankled at the same time. Why should *she* be the one to decide, the only one to admit to desire?

"Do you want me to, Jon?" she asked him frankly.

Suddenly the air was electric between them, charged with a million volts of humming, tingling awareness. Slowly Jon reached for Carole's hand and brought it to his heart. She could feel the rapid beating there.

"God, yes!" he said softly. "I've had a week of rotten nights when I could scarcely sleep for wanting you. I've hardly dared to touch you today—I knew if I did, I couldn't let you go!"

Her heart raced at his honest admission. "I want you, too, Jon," Carole confessed, shaken.

He dropped her hand, executed a perfect U-turn and broke the speed limit all the way to his house.

The moment Jon's door closed behind them, they were in each other's arms. Their mouths fused together—his lips were hot and moist and delicious on hers—and their bodies crushed against one another hungrily. The pounding of Jon's heart against her breast echoed Carole's, and even through their clothes she could feel the hard imprint of his arousal.

"Oh, God, how I want you!" he whispered, his hands running through the waves of her loose, wind-blown hair.

"And I want you!" Urgently Carole's hands explored his shoulders, back and flat waist. "I was so afraid you'd left me again, Jon! That you weren't coming back!"

He threw her a brief puzzled look, then sought the softness of her mouth again. When the kiss deepened Jon shook as though he stood in a strong wind, and this further evidence of his desire enflamed Carole, yet made her feel strangely humble, too. She hadn't known she had such power over him.

His tongue was a honeyed warmth exploring the tenderness of her mouth, increasing her excitement and arousing her almost beyond endurance.

His mouth moved down her throat, then his impatient hands were pulling her knit shirt out of her jeans and the buttons were flying open. Carole had dressed so hastily that morning that she hadn't bothered with a bra. She heard Jon draw in his breath at the sight of her bare breasts, then his mouth fastened over one pink-crested mound, his fingers moving seductively, sensitively, on the other.

He teased her nipple with his tongue, then sucked her whole breast deeply, turning Carole's legs to butter. She gasped with desire, gripping his black head to her yielding chest. Her desire clamored emptily, yearning for his loving invasion.

One large, hasty hand unzipped her jeans, then he was stroking her waist and stomach, his fingers exploring eagerly as far as they could go.

"Jon, I can scarcely stand up," Carole whimpered against the crispness of his hair. Never in her life had she experienced such raw, driving excitement.

"I know just the place for us!"

He drew her through the hall and into his bedroom, where they sprawled across his unmade bed. Gently Jon slid the shirt over Carole's head, then pulled her jeans down her legs. Somehow Carole's own shaky fingers managed to undo his shirt. Her hands went to his small male nipples, and she buried her face in the lovely silken mat of his chest hair while his hands and lips explored her. She cried out in ecstasy when his tongue moved along her inner thighs and writhed while his fingers sensuously stroked and touched her.

I don't know if I can stand such excitement! Carole thought when his thumbs slid beneath the waistband of her panties. She arched her hips to aid him in removing them. Then his hands were beneath her round bottom, exploring and kneading, and what his mouth was doing was so shockingly delightful that she might have been embarrassed had she not also been burning with need.

Her own hands found the zipper of his slacks. It moved down easily, and her impatient fingers slipped within, first to stroke his stomach and navel, then to aid him in removing his own clothes. After they fell beside the bed Jon seized Carole's hands in his, guiding them to his body.

"Please touch me," he breathed in her ear. "I need to feel your soft hands on my skin, on my whole body, Carole."

"I love to touch you, Jon," she replied. She stroked and caressed wherever he had indicated and felt him tense in pleasurable response to her tender touch.

"I can't wait any longer," he choked, his mouth moist against her breast.

"Oh, darling, neither can I," Carole responded.

Without further delay he slipped between her legs. She felt the muscled strength of him seeking, then finding, the heated welcoming core of her. He plunged within, finding his way home, and she gasped against his sweat-slick shoulder.

"You feel so wonderful to me," he whispered. "I'm bathed in the very essence of you, Carole. Oh, such sweet hot flame!"

"*You* feel so wonderful to *me*, Jon," she managed before his lips covered hers again and his tongue plunged into the cavern of her mouth. His deep, hard strokes filled the emptiness of her, easing her aching hunger.

"Give me everything, Carole! I need you so!"

Jon's words drove her wild, left her wanting all of him. At the same time Carole was gripped by the compelling need to give him everything, absolutely everything, he sought from her. She matched his burning movements in perfect, synchronized rhythm, and the exquisite motions of love soon locked them together.

We're like one person, she thought, marveling as her hips, cradled in his hands, rose to meet him. She had never known such utter perfection or such almost unbearable excitement.

Then Carole ceased to think at all and could only cry out in glory and wonder as she was lifted wholly out of her own separate identity and made complete and fulfilled in union with him. Spangles and sunbursts danced before her eyes, then she heard his own joyous cry of fulfillment, timed perfectly with hers.

Lying in the twilight-filled afterglow, Carole relished the feel of Jon's big toe moving lazily across her foot and the warmth of his hair-covered leg against her smooth one. "Guess what?" he said to her teasingly.

She already knew. "Another record recovery time?"

"What you do to my tired, almost middle-aged body is incredible," he murmured against her cheek before sweeping her tightly to him again. "Oh, Carole, my lovely, lovely girl! I never knew a woman could be so desirable—could have a body that matched so perfectly with mine. You satisfy me utterly, then awaken me again. . . ."

When the impassioned words spilled from him, Carole seized him close.

Afterward, they slept contentedly in each other's arms for a lazy hour. Carole stirred once when Jon slipped out of bed, then the drumming of the shower lulled her back to sleep.

She awoke fully when he came back into the room, shaved, scrubbed and sweet-smelling. He wore a navy bathrobe, knotted around his waist, and he tossed a terry wrap to Carole.

"Put this on so you won't distract me and I'll

fix us a drink." His voice held a lightness and buoyancy that thrilled her anew.

Languorously Carole stretched on the rumpled sheets, and Jon's dark eyes glittered, following her every movement. "You don't like being distracted?" she asked seductively.

"You know I love it," he retorted, his mouth softened by a smile. "But I did have something serious to discuss with you. Come join me in the living room."

After Jon left Carole hastily made herself presentable. The terrycloth wrap held the clean scent of him, and she inhaled its fragrance before tying it around her slim body.

In the living room Jon handed her a tall frosted glass and waited until she'd settled herself on the sofa to face him curiously. What was this all about? Carole wondered, a slight feeling of apprehension tightening her throat.

"Carole, I think we ought to get married," Jon said flatly.

She had just taken a sip of her bourbon and water, and she promptly choked on it. Never in her life had she been so startled while filled simultaneously with such a radiant spreading joy.

"Oh, Jon!" Carole breathed when she could speak again. She knew her whole heart full of love must be evident on her glowing face. Then reality crept in. Jon did not look similarly glowing. Rather, he looked almost entirely matter of fact.

"Why do you want to marry me?" Carole said, feeling her apprehension return.

"You should certainly know one of the reasons!" He smiled briefly, then reached over and imprisoned her hand in the vise of his own. "At first I thought if I could just have you *once*—but that once was like throwing logs on a fire. After today I can't bear to let you go!"

"Oh," she said in a small voice. Their ardent, uninhibited lovemaking was certainly a powerful bond, but was it strong enough to hold a marriage together? Carole doubted it.

Jon saw her troubled face. "Don't underestimate what we have, Carole," he said thoughtfully. "It's one of life's miracles when two people make each other feel the way we do! But there's much more to my proposal than sex." He ran a hand through his black hair. "I'm miserable when I'm not with you. I've gotten used to your companionship, to having you ride down the road with me. We've shared so many moments on the book, found things to talk about and laugh over. I don't want that to end." His voice dropped several decibles. "Last week without you was hell!"

"It was for me, too. Oh, Jon, I love you so!" Carole said tremulously, her body throbbing with the enormity of both his words and her own.

For just a fraction of a moment she saw his eyes narrow, saw the surprised, even speculative, glance he threw at her. Then he gave a slow sigh. "You're waiting for me to say, 'I love you, too.' I probably do, Carole. Certainly I can utter those glib words. But I'm going to tell you the truth. Carole, I don't even know what love *means* anymore!"

She went numb with shock at his statement; then chill, icy fingers began to move up and down her spine. Wordlessly Carole stared at Jon. Pain, confusion and honest bewilderment were written on his face.

"Once I thought I knew what love meant," he said after a moment, "but when it ended, there was nothing . . . nothing but such awful, painful memories!"

He must be referring to his late fiancée. Carole knew that if she married Jon, she would have to face the fact that he had once loved someone else. "I—I'd like to hear about that, Jon," she said gamely.

He shook his head. "Raking over the coals of the dead past isn't a good idea."

The chill within her spread. As though he sensed it, Jon drew her back into his arms, warming her with the familiar touch of his body.

"Hey, why don't you make an honest man out of me?" he said teasingly. "Teach me to say those words that come so hard."

"Jon, if you don't love me—" Carole began.

He stopped her by dropping a finger lightly across her lips. "I never said that," he reminded her. "I want you, I need you, I can't imagine life without you. Please say yes!"

She glanced down instead, trying to hang on to

a remnant of common sense. "I have another life—my mother, friends, a career—in Texas."

"You said you found our book of local folklore the most satisfying work you've ever done," he pointed out. "When you've finished this book, other related jobs will come your way. You know they will."

Silently Carole mulled that over. It was true, of course.

"You can do the sort of work you enjoy most and not be overly concerned about money," Jon went on rapidly. "I'm not a poor man, Carole. I've been well paid over the years, and I've made some wise investments."

For a writer, that was a tempting prospect indeed.

"One thing more," he said offhandedly. "Our marriage might stop our relatives from feuding for the first time in centuries. You did say you'd do *anything* to stop the feud!"

"Quit throwing my words back at me," she said almost despairingly, "or trying to buy me, either." God in heaven, what was she to do?

"I'll use any methods I can, I want you so much," Jon threatened. Again his finger brushed her lip, this time caressingly. "Say yes, Carole, or I swear I'll throw you down on this sofa and ravish you repeatedly until you're too weak for any more protests!"

She looked into his beautiful dark eyes. They held laughter mixed with concern and a mysterious glint of something else as well. Why, he really did want to marry her! He was definitely deadly serious about that. Oh, what a difficult, complex, delightful person he was. She loved him and couldn't imagine any sort of life without him.

"Say yes," he urged, his breath warm on her face.

"Yes," Carole whispered. She burrowed her face in the comfortable niche of his neck and shoulder, trying to hide the fact that her throat ached from words unspoken, and her eyes burned with tears unshed. Would he ever come to love her as she loved him? Would he even dare to say it if he did? "He's been hurt so badly," Sally Rodgers had told her.

"Thank you, Carole," Jon said to her softly.

Suddenly the meaning and wonder of this conversation struck her consciousness and sank in. At long, long last Jon Haughton is going to be my husband! Carole thought.

Then Jon pressed his face against her hair and whispered words so poignant that they wrenched her heart. "Oh, Carole, teach me to love again!"

Chapter Eleven

The time was almost up. Carole could soon check the results of the test and then she'd know for sure. But now that the moment of truth was upon her, her heart tightened with fear. How was it possible to want something so badly—yet not want it, too?

Nervously she glanced at the watch on her left wrist. Yes, the time was up. When Carole lowered her hand, she saw the shining glint of her wide gold wedding ring.

She had worn that ring for six weeks. Only three days after she and Jon returned from the Great Smoky Mountains with Betsy and Terry, they had been married. The younger couple had been their only attendants—indeed the only people present except for the Presbyterian minister and his beaming wife. Because Carole had preferred a religious ceremony, she and Jon had stood within a small red-brick church on a hilltop to exchange the solemn vows that made them man and wife—in the world's eyes, at least. Down deep in her heart, where a new source of pain had sprung up and grown steadily in strength, Carole knew that she had never been Jon's wife, regardless of the ceremony or the words on their marriage license.

Until they were married they had told absolutely no one except Betsy and Terry of their intentions. Then, once the marriage was an accomplished fact, they announced it to both families.

Carole had called her mother first and listened to Marsha Coldren's tearful exclamations of joy. "Oh, darling, how wonderful! Is your husband the same man you've always loved?" she asked.

"How did you know I've always loved someone?" Carole asked, astounded by her mother's astuteness.

"How could I not know it," Marsha countered, "when you came dragging home from North Carolina looking like the world had ended before you were eighteen!"

"I married that same man," Carole assured her.

"Oh, darling, now you'll be happy at last. I know you will!"

Happy? Oh, yes, in the first flush of wedded life she had been blissfully happy. Even the rival families had appeared to rejoice. At the Coldrens' there were handclasps for Jon and kisses for Carole. Aunt Eugenia had declared herself overjoyed, and even crusty Pop Arnold Haughton pronounced the news, "Mighty fine." If the families thought or said anything else in private, they put their best face forward for the newlyweds.

Jon's astounded family had been entirely welcoming to Carole, too. In the lush, green valley where his parents lived in a modern farmhouse, Jon's sweet-faced mother shed tears of joy. "Oh, my dear, I've so wanted him to marry and I'd begun to think he never would!"

"I hope you'll be very, very happy, Carole," said Jon's courtly, still strikingly handsome, white-haired father.

Jon's brothers and sisters had all been cordial, too, with the sole exception of Sally. She looked distressed even as she mouthed her own best wishes.

Oh, no one tolled church bells or gathered all the kinfolk together for a glorious celebration. A Coldren-Haughton marriage was still something to be treated rather gingerly. Yet no one was running for their rifles, either, as Carole pointed out in a letter to her mother.

Dr. Thomas Kaufman and Lois Wyler were simply and genuinely happy. "It's the beginning of a whole new era," Tom declared at the festive dinner for four when he and Lois feted the newlyweds. Small silver wedding bells decorated the tablecloth, a bottle of champagne was promptly uncorked and Lois served a traditional and delicious white cake for dessert.

But even as they talked and laughed and sipped champagne, the first uneasy stirrings that hinted at disaster were awakening within Carole.

Her disquiet began with the realization that Jon was carefully closemouthed around her. Although Carole knew from his work schedule that progress on the dam had accelerated, she had been told very little about it and had not even visited the site until Willie Running-Brook arrived for a brief postwedding visit. To Willie, Jon spoke enthusiastically of his work, and he drove his friend out to the site. At least Carole was allowed to accompany them to the headwaters of the Hilamunga River, but Jon's attention wasn't focused on her as he spoke of stress factors and flood control measures and other things that Carole understood not at all.

Jon also seemed evasive on the subject of whether or not he and Carole should have children. "I think that's more your decision than mine," he remarked. "You'd be the one most tied down by the tending and caring. You know how busy I am."

That was certainly no answer to Carole's eager questions.

Nor were those the only incidents. Twice Jon was guilty of verbal slips, introducing his bride as "Carole Coldren," although he knew she had decided to take his name.

From the very beginning he had mystified her more than ever. Although *he* had pressed for this marriage, before three weeks were over Carole knew he was not truly comfortable in it.

Not that he was unkind, not at all! Clearly Jon hadn't married her to hurt or punish her. Rather, he was still her constant, ardent lover, and their nights in each other's arms were perfection. Had he been any other man in the world,

Carole would have believed that the husband who kissed her so readily and whispered extravagant, impassioned words when they made love adored her completely.

And perhaps he did. But he didn't trust her.

She sensed that there was something that pushed and drove him relentlessly. She knew he didn't want to smash their fragile relationship, that he wanted her in his home, in his bed and in his arms, but something he would not or could not name forced him on.

Sometimes he came home unexpectedly during the day. He always found Carole working, for the book on the feud was going quite well. Although she wanted to believe that Jon simply needed a map he'd forgotten to take to the office, in her heart Carole realized the truth: He was checking up on her.

Jon was like a man with a desirable mistress, yet one he trusted not a whit. He seemed to anticipate betrayal, and, agonizingly, Carole wondered why. What on earth provoked him to hold her in such low esteem? She was a dependable, truthful, trustworthy person, she always had been! Or did he distrust her simply because she'd been born a Coldren? Was the feud to flourish anew in a private and personal setting?

"You're destroying us, don't you know that?" she longed to cry at him. But what were the specifics she could cite? A slip of the tongue? A forgotten map? No, she could not put her complaints into words, for they sounded too petty.

But their cumulative effect was devastating to her.

Now her very own moment of truth had come.

She still loved Jon—she always would. He was the sun around which her world revolved. The six weeks Carole had spent with him, and all the lovely nights when she'd lain in his arms, left her bound to him. Sometimes when she glanced at his strong handsome face and magnificent body, thinking, "My husband!," her heart squeezed so tightly that the proud joy was close to pain.

"Oh, my love, my darling, my only, only one," she had heard herself whispering to him several nights ago when they'd last made love.

Carole pushed herself up from the table where she'd waited through several long and seemingly endless hours. She walked to the phone and placed a call. Moments later she slumped into her chair again, emotion leaden in her stomach.

She was pregnant, as she had suspected.

A wave of conflicting emotions struck her so suddenly that she had to lean on the table for support. Joy that she would bear Jon's child mingled with the grief of knowing she would lose its father.

Once, just a few short weeks ago, she had sat in a log cabin and heard an old man of almost ninety speak of his childhood, of the distrust and hatred that had sprung up between his parents. Their loveless marriage and silent feud had culminated in terrible tragedy and the spilling of innocent blood. It had haunted him for the rest of his life.

Moaning softly, Carole buried her face in her hands.

She could not allow a child of hers and Jon's to go through even one day of the sort of life Arnold Haughton had known. From the moment she first suspected she was pregnant, Carole had vowed that. Yet how could she bear to leave the man who had given her this baby? Her body trembled uncontrollably in powerful, silent resistance. Never again to taste his kisses, feel his touch and lose herself in the strong, earthy passion they shared! How could she endure such a penance?

She would endure it because she had to. Hadn't she herself been raised by a single parent who was fortified by loving memories? Certainly that was better, Carole knew, than to find herself growing hard and embittered by Jon's lack of faith in her.

Dimly she heard the sound of a bell ringing in the background—the front doorbell. She determined to ignore it. She was in no shape to face anyone just now, for hot tears were beginning to splash down her face.

In Texas she would have her mother's help, Carole thought. Together they could raise Jon's child to be as he'd been once—happy and open-hearted, loving and trusting. Would the baby be a boy? Oh, she prayed it would! A boy with his father's dark hair and eyes, his fine-featured face and lithe, graceful steps.

The doorbell rang again. Carole flinched but refused to stir from her chair.

She would tell no one about the baby until she was safely back in Houston. Later, of course, she would have to let Jon know. He would probably prove quite a good absent parent. The child could spend summers with him here in North Carolina. . . .

For her, it would all be quite terrible. She would be so desolate without Jon. . . .

"Carole? Carole, are you in there?"

Oh, God, that was Susan's voice! Obviously the woman had walked around to the side door and was proceeding to pound on it. Susan would have seen Carole's car in the drive and she wouldn't give up easily, not Susan with her wide streak of curiosity and her eternal nosy questions.

Reluctantly Carole dried her eyes, got up and walked to the door. Sighing, she pushed back the lock and allowed the door to swing open.

"Hi," Susan greeted her. "I was passing by and since I've hardly seen you since you and Jon got married—" Her voice broke off. Her thin, sharp face went still. "Carole, what's wrong?"

Carole stepped back and Susan came inside.

"Carole, what's happened? You look ghastly! Where is Jon—?"

"He was called to Raleigh again, day before yesterday. Something to do with the dam. He comes back tonight."

"What's happened to you?" Susan persisted. "Something has, I know!"

So she was to have no easy reprieve. They would all have to know soon enough, Coldrens and Haughtons alike. What better time to start preparing them than now?

"Susan, I'm leaving Jon," Carole said tersely and felt a fresh splatter of tears against her cheeks. "This just isn't working out."

"Oh, no!" Her cousin's small face went white and pinched. "Carole, has Jon been mean to you? Has he—?"

"No! He's never raised a hand to me. You're certainly not looking at an abused wife." Carole took a breath, trying to steady herself, for she knew she must be careful not to fan the flames of old hatreds. "He's been very good to me. Susan, you must make sure everyone understands *that* about Jon."

"Then, why?"

"I can't discuss it. Just, please . . . go!" Carole turned and walked into the bedroom she shared with Jon. She opened the huge walk-in closet and reached for one of her empty suitcases.

Susan followed her, seizing Carole's arm and swinging her around. "Why?" she said agonizedly. "Oh, Carole, you *must* tell me!"

Even through her own misery, Carole was startled by the depth of emotion in her cousin's quaking voice. Why should Susan care so?

"He doesn't trust me. He doesn't really love me," she blurted, unable to bottle up her feelings any longer. "I suppose it's because I'm a Coldren. Now let go of me, Susan. I've got to pack."

There would never be a better chance for her to leave Green Grove than right now, while Jon was still out of town.

Susan's face turned paper white. "Carole, what has Jon ever told you . . . about the past?"

Carole looked at her in mild surprise. "Practically nothing. He refuses to discuss it. I've told you that."

Susan drew a breath so deep that her thin chest heaved. "Carole, I'll go now," she said, speaking very quietly and distinctly, "but I'll be back in less than an hour with Reggie. Wait for us. Oh, Carole, there's something you *must* know."

She knew all she needed to know and it was breaking her heart, killing her by small degrees.

"Carole, promise me you won't leave till I've come back with Reggie!" Susan's fingers clutched like talons, biting into Carole's arm.

"It will take me an hour to pack," Carole said, trying to ignore a small, wavering uncertainty. She didn't care what Susan thought. Nor did she know why she should see Reggie, of all people. Yet there was a very strange look on Susan's face.

Susan scooted for the door, and Carole heard her letting herself out. All right, she'd wait for them, but what great secret did they expect to impart? That Susan and Reggie had once gone to Uncle Buck Coldren? Carole already knew that.

Blindly she reached into the closet and pulled out an armload of clothes. Her new blue silk dress lay on top. It had a fitted bodice and simple elegant lines. Carole had bought the dress for her wedding. Jon had worn his dove gray suit. Her hands found that in the closet, and for a moment she buried her face in the folds of his coat. Jon's scent hovered there. Finally Carole forced herself to pull away.

She had finished packing her clothes and cosmetics when she heard a car door slam outside.

A moment later the voice she longed above all to hear, yet feared most, floated toward her from the living room. "Carole, I'm home early. Carole?"

"Jon!" Even as her heart thudded in the sudden guilty realization of knowing herself discovered, resentment brimmed, too, in Carole's breast. Had he really gotten back early, or had he deliberately misled her about the time of his return?

"Carole, where are you?"

"Here," she called swiftly, stepping out of the bedroom and closing the door on her packed suitcases.

Jon set down his briefcase and a couple of rolled maps, then turned to regard her. "Why, you're not dressed yet." His gaze took in the long, flowered patio dress Carole wore, and he smiled, as though realizing she had nothing on beneath it. "Come over here," he invited, his eyes taking on the smoky hue that she knew was a prelude to lovemaking.

She couldn't bear to touch him, or she knew she would be lost in the haven of his arms. While

Carole hesitated she heard another car pull up outside and stop. Jon heard it, too, for he turned with a frown, his arms dropping to his sides.

"That's Susan," Carole said quickly. "She was over here earlier. She and Reggie have something to tell me." All at once her knees began trembling, and she sank down on the sofa.

She saw Jon's quizzical look turn to surprise and then concern. "Are you all right, Carole? You look so pale."

The doorbell chimed and Carole made a helpless motion with her hand. She felt too weak to move. What would Jon say or do when he discovered that she planned to leave him? Carole had no hope of being able to conceal that fact from him for very long.

His face darkening with sudden suspicion, Jon hurried to answer the door. She heard the brief flurry of conversation from the entry hall.

"Glad you're back," Susan murmured.

"What's going on, anyway?" Jon said sharply.

"There's something Carole should have known about long ago. We've come here to tell her." Reggie's voice sounded just as heavy as Carole's heart felt.

They all entered the living room. "Sit down," Jon said automatically.

Susan's face looked even more pinched, if that were possible. "I don't think you'll want us to, Jon, not when you hear what we've come to say. But I can't let Carole leave you without telling her the truth."

"Carole *leave* me. What—?" Jon leaned back

against the mantel as though all his strength had suddenly drained away. Carole braced herself for the angry accusation in his eyes, but they were blank, stunned by the impact of Susan's words.

"Why?" he breathed after a very long moment had passed.

He still stared at Susan, not at Carole, but she saw the involuntary tremor that ran through his legs, saw his face go a ghastly gray color, as though all the blood had just drained from his heart.

Suddenly he no longer mystified Carole. Perhaps knowing that his baby nestled within her body had attuned her to him, for she understood that look on his face. Why, he loved her! No man could look like that unless he was threatened with the loss of what was most precious to him.

"Jon," Carole heard herself whispering.

He turned to face her, his color still ashen, his face stricken with pain. "Why?" he said again.

Susan answered before Carole could speak. "She says you don't trust her, Jon, but she doesn't understand why and it's breaking her heart. She loves you so much!"

Jon drew a ragged breath. Carole saw him swallow hard, but he didn't deny the truth of Susan's charge.

Susan swung around to look again at Carole, and torment was evident in her brown eyes. "You don't know what happened eleven years ago." Her voice was little more than a whisper. "Jon did come back from working on that bridge

—he came back to meet you. He went to Morgan's Cove."

"He went to meet me—" Carole repeated over the heavy thudding of her heart. Then comprehension sank in.

"We were waiting for him instead." Now Reggie was the one who spoke. "Oh, I didn't know what was going to happen. Blake Coldren and a friend of his, Al Grayson, had recruited me to join them."

"I don't understand," Carole whispered, her heart still beating ominously. Al Grayson had later become Wynne Coldren's first husband, she remembered fleetingly.

"I was the new guy in town and I was crazy in love with Susan," Reggie went on, his expression hangdog. "I wanted to get in good with her family. Blake said that one of the Haughtons—Jon—had gotten too forward with Carole. He and Al planned to teach Jon a lesson. I didn't realize what they had in mind until they put on ski masks and tossed one to me."

For a moment Carole's heart seemed to stop completely, while her eyes flew to her husband. Jon was beginning to recover from his earlier shock, but his face was grim as he heard the other man's confession.

"So you were one of them," Jon said, his voice dangerously soft. "I always thought so, but, of course, I couldn't prove it. It was too dark. Blake was the only one I recognized."

"Jon, what did they do to you?" Carole hardly

recognized the cry as her own, torn from her terror-filled throat.

"They grabbed me, pinned my arms behind my back and threw me into Blake's truck," Jon said, his voice devoid of expression. "They carried me up into the mountains and beat the hell out of me. They came within an inch of killing me."

At his words, a sob escaped Susan and her fist went to her mouth.

"You fought like the very devil," Reggie said heavily to Jon. "If there hadn't been three of us, we never could have done it." He swung back to face Carole. "Finally we got Jon down on the ground. Blake panicked. He broke a rock over Jon's head. We heard a—a terrible cracking sound. God, I thought for sure we'd killed you!"

"You damn near did," Jon said unemotionally, but livid color stained his cheekbones, in sharp contrast to the earlier grayness of his face.

"When Jon went so limp and still we didn't know what to do," Reggie went on. "I was scared sick. The others were, too. Finally Blake said, 'We'd better throw him in the creek.' So we did . . . and drove off hell for leather. It had all gotten out of hand. We hadn't intended . . . We thought we'd done murder!"

Susan lowered her shaking hands from her mouth, but she, too, faced Carole squarely. "Now you know why Jon never came back to you," she said with a gulping sob. "He didn't dump you, Carole. He didn't come back because he couldn't!"

"Jon . . ." Carole stared at her husband, trying to understand all that she'd been told, but her mind was too stunned by the recent series of events to function properly.

His bleak eyes met hers. "So you really didn't know what they did," he said to her thinly. "I—I've always hoped you didn't, Carole. When you came back to Green Grove, when I saw that same sweetness and honesty in you . . ." His shoulders heaved with resignation. "You were so young eleven years ago. I guess when you set up that meeting at Morgan's Cove, you thought they'd just *talk* to me."

Sudden illumination shot through Carole's numbed brain. "Jon, what do you mean? I didn't set anything up!"

His face went ashen once again. "Your letter said . . ."

"Yes, I wrote you a letter," she agreed distractedly.

"Jon, you never got *Carole's* letter." Susan was sobbing openly now. She fumbled in the handbag she carried and drew out a small envelope. Once it had been white, but now it was yellowed with age.

"I've saved it all these years," Susan wept. "It's been the reminder of my guilt. You see . . . Wynne was so furious and jealous that you had chosen Carole and not her. She told me that Blake just intended to 'teach Jon a lesson about messing around with Coldren girls.' Wynne said if I didn't help her, she—she'd take Reggie away from me!"

"She couldn't have," Reggie interrupted.

"I know that now. I didn't then. I was so scared of Wynne! So when I saw the letter that Carole put in the box to be mailed to you, Jon, I took it. I read it to Wynne. Then she and Blake told me to write another letter, the one that would lure you to Morgan's Cove. God help me, I did it!"

Susan broke down sobbing, and Jon sprang away from the mantel and seized her thin shoulders. "You!" he choked. Then he asked in disbelief, "You mean Carole didn't even know about this?"

"Carole has never known a thing about *any* of this until now. Oh, Jon, just look at her!"

Numbly Carole raised her face, not knowing what was written there, but something—something he read caused Jon's own face to crumble. Briefly his eyes went wild. "Do you know what you've done?" he cried to Susan. "I worshiped Carole! I planned to marry her. She was the whole world to me!"

"Yes, I know!" Susan screamed back. "I've lived with it every day for eleven years! Every time my husband touched me, I'd think about it. About you and Carole. Both still so alone. Both unmarried. It's—it's practically killed me! I knew when I first urged Carole to come back here to Green Grove, to tackle Tom Kaufman's project, that all this would probably come out— that it had to, no matter what it cost Reggie and me. Because it's ruined our marriage and been killing us by slow degrees!"

Jon's hands dropped from Susan's shoulders. Only his eyes looked alive. "May I have my letter?"

Susan handed it to him. Jon opened the two sheets of dried, crackling paper and scanned them rapidly. Then the sheets fluttered from his hand while he walked, ever so slowly, to Carole.

She still sat on the sofa, unable to move.

Jon dropped on his knees before her. He took her lifeless hands in his. "Carole, can you ever forgive me?"

His agonized words snapped the terrible spell holding her in thrall, and Carole saw the stark pain on Jon's face. Slowly she drew her hands from his while he waited, like a prisoner, for whatever she might do next.

Carole's trembling hands went to either side of his face. "You—you really thought *I'd* been part of that terrible thing that happened to you?" she asked incredulously.

"Yes. No. I mean, you weren't there to meet me at the cove, but they were. What was I to think?" She saw the shudder of his shoulders, his terrible battle against the pain of his memories. "But, no, in a way I must have always known you were innocent. My heart knew. All you've ever had to do is smile at me and I—I melt inside. My body knew, too. I couldn't help wanting you—I've always wanted you. It was just my mind—my hard, logical, remorseless mind. . . ." For a moment his voice faded. "Carole, can you ever forgive me?"

242

A door slammed. Susan and Reggie, having told the truth at last, had fled.

"Oh, Jon, I could forgive you anything! Don't you know how much I love you?" Carole whispered.

Her words and the look on her face undid him completely. A hard sob broke from his lips as he gathered her to his chest. "I do now!" he said, holding and rocking her like a child. Long, long moments passed while they clung together, their arms entwined, pressing as close to each other as possible.

"Tell me . . ." Carole said at last.

"Anything!" Jon raised his face to look at her, his eyes naked with pain.

"What happened to you after they . . . they left you there?"

"I was unconscious." Jon spoke swiftly. "When I finally started coming to, my head felt like it was broken and my whole body was on fire from the beating. I had a bad concussion—I saw everything with double vision. I fell down three or four times before I got my balance.

"I didn't know where I was," he continued painfully. "I don't even remember much about the next two days when I was stumbling around, trying to find my way out of the woods. I was so weak and sick from exposure, if I hadn't finally blundered into a group of road surveyors, I would have died. They rushed me to a hospital in a little town north of here." His body shook with the terrible memories. "Carole, it all happened a long time ago. You don't want to hear any——"

"Tell me!" she insisted, her hands gripping his shoulders.

"All right. Even with good medical attention, it was still touch and go for a couple of days. By the time I was able to tell the doctors who I was, my family had just started searching for me. They were so used to my comings and goings, nobody got excited at first."

"Why didn't you have them arrested and tried for attempted murder?" Carole demanded, her voice quaking now from fury as well as pain.

"First, I didn't know for sure who the others were. I couldn't even prove Blake had been the ringleader." Jon's arms tightened around Carole. "Second, I knew there could only be more trouble, more bloodshed, if I did speak out. My family guessed the truth, and they wanted revenge, but they—they did what I wanted." One of his long, slim hands reached up to smooth Carole's tousled hair. "Oh, my darling, don't look like that! It's all over."

"No." She sensed that there was still something he was holding back. Her fingers plucked at him urgently. "Tell me the rest, Jon."

"That was the very worst," he admitted softly. "When I was discharged from the hospital I went to Sally's house in Green Grove to continue recuperating. One night—the first night I could stand up and walk any distance—I went out the back door. I still couldn't entirely believe what I thought you'd done. I headed for your Uncle

Paul's house. But one of Buck Coldren's deputies was parked up the street. He stopped me before I got there and called on the car radio for Buck. I guess when Blake and Wynne found out I was still alive they told their father some vague version of what had happened. Since Buck was afraid there might be more trouble, he'd been watching your house.

"I'd wanted to see you, Carole, one more time, just to ask why? Why did you set me up? But, of course, I never got to see you. There was just Buck with his pistol and that damned revolving blue light."

Carole's mind flew back to that same night, when she'd been thinking of Jon, too. When, looking from her window, she'd seen the sheriff's blue-lighted car parked beneath her window. A burglar, she'd been told.

"Buck put me in his car and delivered a little speech," Jon went on. "He was sorry I'd gotten 'roughed-up.' Then he told me how really young you were. Seventeen. 'Jailbait'—that was his word. I—I was so shocked, Carole, and I was still so weak from the injuries that I lost all sense of perspective."

"My age that summer was the only lie I've ever told you, Jon!" she cried.

He nodded, believing her. "Anyway, Buck drove me over to Sally's and let me go with a warning to stay away from you. When he drove off, I went haywire. I remember I fell across the lawn, cursing you, calling you terrible names. It was like all the light in my life had gone out.

245

Sally had been watching for me. She was almost out of her mind with worry. She saw me—heard me. Came out and held me while I prayed I'd die. I never knew anything could hurt so badly as thinking you hated me, that you'd had them waiting for me—not once, but twice." He drew an uneven breath. "That's it. That's all. In the years since, I tried to excuse you by saying you were just a kid then, but, down deep, I guess I couldn't forgive you. Now try to forgive *me!*"

Carole thought of the brokenhearted young man he'd been, and her tears came in a flood. She wept both for Jon and herself, for the bitter unjust memories they'd each held of the other, and all the long, wasted years.

"Darling, darling, don't cry so!" Jon begged her, but Carole's tears came from a flood of grief too strong to stem.

"Sweetheart, it's over—it's over at last! Come with me—come lie down," Jon said urgently, but when he tried to help Carole off the sofa her knees buckled.

He swept her into his strong arms and carried her back to their bedroom, stopping only to open the door. Then Jon laid her down gently on their bed and sat beside her, stroking her hair and her grief-contorted face.

"Carole, can I get you—?"

"No, just hold me, Jon. Please!" she managed in a strangled voice.

"Oh, my darling! My own lost love that I've found again," he whispered. He gathered her against him, pillowing her head on his broad chest. Gradually, consoled by his arms and the strong rapid beat of his heart against hers, Carole's tears began to slow.

"When I think how they hurt you!" she cried.

"Don't think of that!" Jon commanded. "Do you know what *I'm* thinking about? That you always loved me, and it's like an old wound has healed at last! I'm whole again. I'm happy. And I know how very, very much I love you, Carole Haughton!"

As his words sank in she drew back a little to gaze at him wonderingly and saw what she'd never expected or dared to hope to see again. Despite the storm of emotions that had wracked them both, Jon's eyes meeting hers were bright, serene and brimming over with love—for her.

While she stared at him he gave her a slow smile. It held the depth of sweetness and trust that she'd seen on the face of the man she'd loved eleven years ago and had despaired of ever seeing again. Her old lover had returned, her tender, passionate Jon.

He's going to look at me like this for the rest of our lives! Carole marveled. "Oh, how I love you!" she murmured.

They came together, moving instinctively toward each other, their lips meeting and clinging until Jon drew back a mere inch. His eyes had stopped on Carole's two suitcases. "Susan said you were going to leave me. I couldn't blame you if you did! I knew how badly I was treating you. But at the same time I wanted you so much I was deathly afraid of losing you. Sometimes, when I came home, it was just to be sure you were still here, still with me."

Carole couldn't bear hearing that she'd caused him even one moment's further torment. "I'll stay—I'll stay as long as you want me, Jon."

"Then you'll stay forever!" he said fiercely. His mouth sought and found her willing, receptive one, and the familiar fire of passion suddenly flared between them again.

"Carole, my sweetheart, my lover, my wife—" She heard him stop, then came his audible, wondering intake of breath. *"My wife!"*

He had never called her that before. When she heard Jon say that simple, beautiful word, Carole felt herself opening to him as she had never done before. Her mind, heart and body all fused into a single, total gift to him. "My husband!" she whispered back, caressing him with hands as eager and loving as his while she sought to give him everything.

Later, much later, after they had made love, Jon helped her unpack her suitcases and put them away. Then they went back to bed and lay there naked to laugh and talk and touch each other joyously.

"You have to be the most remarkable woman in the world," Jon marveled, looking down on Carole's flushed face with incredible tenderness. "Even after you thought I'd ditched you years ago, you could still look at me and say, 'I love you.'"

"I don't think that's so remarkable," Carole retorted gently, pushing back a lock of the crisp black hair that had tumbled across his forehead. "You thought I was partially responsible for nearly killing you, but you still asked me to marry you. Now I call *that* remarkable!"

"Sounds like two crazy people crazy in love with each other." He smiled.

"Jon?" A wisp of thought ran through Carole's mind. "Were you ever engaged to a girl after we broke up?"

"Me? Lord, no!" he said emphatically. "Oh, there were girls . . . women. You know I haven't been an angel. But there's only been one I ever really loved. Why?"

"The first day I came back to Green Grove, Terry told me . . ." She related what the boy had said.

"I can't imagine. Oh!" A thoughtful look crossed his handsome face. "Once, when Terry was about ten, I was back here visiting between jobs. Sally and I were talking privately. She asked me if I still loved you. I remember I told her that as far as I was concerned you were dead and buried. It still wasn't true, but I guess I was trying to convince myself. Anyway, we looked up and saw Terry standing in the door. I suppose Sally made up a lie for Terry about my having had a fiancée who died."

"Maybe Sally won't dislike me so much now," Carole whispered, trailing her lips across his bare shoulder.

"Once she knows what actually happened eleven years ago, she'll love you. She's a loving person," Jon assured her.

Carole nestled against him, and his lips brushed her forehead. "What are you thinking, Jon?" she asked, savoring this sharing of their hearts. It was just as wonderful in its way as the sharing of their bodies.

"That I love you. That if you and I hadn't been interfered with, we would have been married for years by now. Why, the way I felt about you, we'd have had a whole yard full of kids!"

Carole looked up at him anxiously. "Would you like children, Jon?"

"Yes, very much. Would you, Carole?" He looked at her in such an eager, hopeful way that her heart did a gleeful somersault.

"Only if they're yours," she said, sliding her arms up and around his neck. "Oh, Jon! I want a little boy with black hair—"

"Then we'll have to have at least two," he responded, "because I absolutely insist on a girl with her mama's bright hair and big brown eyes." He laughed, the sound so youthful, happy and free that her heart soared. "What the heck! Even though we're getting a late start, let's fill up the yard with our own blend of Coldrens and Haughtons. I can't think of a better end to a stupid feud!"

"You'll have to make the first announcement to our kinfolk quite soon!" Carole smiled back at him, and then, as Jon looked down at her quizzically, then with the sudden dawning of delighted understanding, she drew his face back to hers and whispered the secret that ended, for all times, their own personal feud.

MORE ROMANCE FOR
A SPECIAL WAY TO RELAX
$1.95 each

2 ☐ Hastings	21 ☐ Hastings	41 ☐ Halston	60 ☐ Thorne
3 ☐ Dixon	22 ☐ Howard	42 ☐ Drummond	61 ☐ Beckman
4 ☐ Vitek	23 ☐ Charles	43 ☐ Shaw	62 ☐ Bright
5 ☐ Converse	24 ☐ Dixon	44 ☐ Eden	63 ☐ Wallace
6 ☐ Douglass	25 ☐ Hardy	45 ☐ Charles	64 ☐ Converse
7 ☐ Stanford	26 ☐ Scott	46 ☐ Howard	65 ☐ Cates
8 ☐ Halston	27 ☐ Wisdom	47 ☐ Stephens	66 ☐ Mikels
9 ☐ Baxter	28 ☐ Ripy	48 ☐ Ferrell	67 ☐ Shaw
10 ☐ Thiels	29 ☐ Bergen	49 ☐ Hastings	68 ☐ Sinclair
11 ☐ Thornton	30 ☐ Stephens	50 ☐ Browning	69 ☐ Dalton
12 ☐ Sinclair	31 ☐ Baxter	51 ☐ Trent	70 ☐ Clare
13 ☐ Beckman	32 ☐ Douglass	52 ☐ Sinclair	71 ☐ Skillern
14 ☐ Keene	33 ☐ Palmer	53 ☐ Thomas	72 ☐ Belmont
15 ☐ James	35 ☐ James	54 ☐ Hohl	73 ☐ Taylor
16 ☐ Carr	36 ☐ Dailey	55 ☐ Stanford	74 ☐ Wisdom
17 ☐ John	37 ☐ Stanford	56 ☐ Wallace	75 ☐ John
18 ☐ Hamilton	38 ☐ John	57 ☐ Thornton	76 ☐ Ripy
19 ☐ Shaw	39 ☐ Milan	58 ☐ Douglass	77 ☐ Bergen
20 ☐ Musgrave	40 ☐ Converse	59 ☐ Roberts	78 ☐ Gladstone

Silhouette Special Edition

MORE ROMANCE FOR
A SPECIAL WAY TO RELAX

$2.25 each

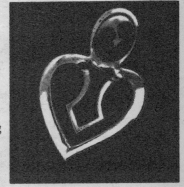

If you enjoyed this book...

...you will enjoy a Special Edition Book Club membership even more.

It will bring you each new title, as soon as it is published every month, delivered right to your door.

15-Day Free Trial Offer

We will send you 6 new Silhouette Special Editions to keep for 15 days absolutely free! If you decide not to keep them, send them back to us, you pay nothing. But if you enjoy them as much as we think you will, keep them and pay the invoice enclosed with your trial shipment. You will then automatically become a member of the Special Edition Book Club and receive 6 more romances every month. There is no minimum number of books to buy and you can cancel at any time.

693-1557

Get the Silhouette Books Newsletter every month for a year.

Now you can receive the fascinating and infor-mative Silhouette Books Newsletter 12 times a year. Every issue is packed with inside information about your favorite Silhouette authors, upcoming books, and a variety of entertaining features—including the authors' favorite romantic recipes, quizzes on plots and characters, and articles about the locales featured in Silhouette books. Plus contests where you can win terrific prizes.

The Silhouette Books Newsletter has been available only to Silhouette Home Subscribers. Now you, too, can enjoy the Newsletter all year long for just $19.95. Enter your subscription now, so you won't miss a single exciting issue.

Silhouette Books